ECO-KIDS
THE

THE GREEN TEAM

Other Books in the
ECO-KIDS *Series*
from Avon Camelot by
Kathryn Makris

KATHRYN MAKRIS is the author of seventeen Young Adult and middle grades novels, including the ALMOST SISTERS series and CROSSTOWN from Avon Books.

As a reporter, Kathryn has covered hurricanes, capital murder trials, and Lego contests. She has hosted a radio talk show and has interviewed national personalities including the Rev. Jesse Jackson, Sissy Spacek, the real "Colonel" Sanders, and Benji the dog.

Raised in Texas in a family that spoke Greek and Spanish along with English, Kathryn now thrives on California's mix of cultures. She also enjoys flamenco dance, dogs, and almost anything outdoors.

THE ECO-KIDS

THE GREEN TEAM

KATHRYN MAKRIS

AN AVON CAMELOT BOOK

THE ECO-KIDS 3: THE GREEN TEAM is an original publication of Avon Books. This work has never before appeared in book form. Any similarity to actual persons or events is purely coincidental.

AVON BOOKS
A division of
The Hearst Corporation
1350 Avenue of the Americas
New York, New York 10019

Copyright © 1994 by Kathryn Makris
Published by arrangement with the author
Library of Congress Catalog Card Number: 93-90664
ISBN: 0-380-77051-2
RL: 5.0

First Avon Camelot Printing: April 1994

CAMELOT TRADEMARK REG. U.S. PAT. OFF. AND IN OTHER COUNTRIES, MARCA REGISTRADA, HECHO EN U.S.A.

Printed in the U.S.A.

OPM   10 9 8 7 6 5 4 3 2 1

This book is dedicated to:

My mother, sister and Gavin for seeing me through;

My enormously patient editors at Avon Books;

"Eco-kids" S. Frost, M.B. Mitchell, B. O'Connor,
K. Rambo, and J. Wiesenfeld,
activists in the best sense of the word and
dear friends who helped THE ECO-KIDS
books come to be.

For their enthusiasm and generosity with time and information, thanks to Betsy Cutler at the California Academy of Sciences in San Francisco, California, and to the many helpful staff members at the U.S. Fish and Wildlife Service.

1

"Come on, move it! Pick up your feet! We're never gonna get there!" Like a sheepdog nipping at his flock, a boy in a baseball cap darted in and out of the big jumble of kids walking down Jewel Beach.

When he bumped into Sienna Sabo, she shoved back. That, she had learned, was the best way to deal with Ramon Sanchez and other unruly boys.

Today she didn't feel like dealing with him at all. For this Eco-kids picnic she was missing a special Saturday coaching session in her drama club. It was one o'clock, too, absolutely the worst time to be on the beach. Her skin would fry and freckle if she didn't keep her sleeves down, collar up, and sunscreen thick.

"Take it easy," she told Ramon, repositioning the big straw hat protecting her auburn curls. "What's your rush, anyway?"

"Good question." Her friend Cary Chen nodded, making her short black hair bob. "This is a whale-watching picnic, Ramon, not a military march."

He waved his arms. The brisk January wind caught at the black bangs that poked out from under his San Diego Padres cap. "I'm starving, that's the rush. The

1

longer it takes to get to China Hill, the later we'll eat."

Sienna rolled her eyes. At the last Eco-kids meeting in the headquarters in Cary's garage, Ramon and Derek Han had put away an entire package of cinnamon rolls. None of it seemed to stick to Ramon's ribby frame, but he was growing taller, getting close to Sienna's height, and she was one of the tallest kids in their seventh grade class.

"If you didn't burn so many calories acting hyper," Jess McCabe told him, "you wouldn't be hungry so often."

Leave it to Jess to explain it scientifically.

Jogging backward, Ramon grinned. "But I'm a growing boy."

Like Sienna, Cary, and Jess, Ramon was one of the Eco-kids' oldest members. One of the original ones, in fact, dating back from the days last summer when they were still called the Five Cat Club. Webb Marsh made the fifth member.

Nowadays there were tons of new ones. Sienna glanced around at the rest of the group. Nate Mackey, a wiry, compact surfer. Sheela Chopra, a sweet sixth-grader from their old elementary school. Hefty Hallie Greer, the girls' star basketball forward at Jewel Beach Junior High. Some came from other schools and neighborhoods, having heard about the Eco-kids and Eco-juniors through news reports.

It was kind of exciting being part of such a big group. Maybe it wasn't so bad to be with them instead of with the drama club. Anyway, she never would have heard the end of it from Cary and Jess if she hadn't attended the Eco-kids' first official picnic. The three of them had started the group last summer when they'd rescued a litter of abandoned kittens in their neighborhood. They'd worked hard and had fun, too. Sienna remembered the sweet feeling of bottle-feeding the kittens in Cary's den last summer. Later they introduced one of them to Jess's grandmother, who fell in love with it and talked Jess's mother into adopting it. Then came the day when Cary and Jess helped convince Sienna's parents that she should have a kitten, too.

Sienna had to admit that it felt good to spend today—a special Eco-kids day—with her friends.

She decided to think about missing the drama club session in a different way. It was called "positive imaging," a method she had learned during a special class she'd taken with her parents. If you started thinking of something negative as something positive, the instructor had said, it could quickly become positive.

She turned to Kristin Capelli, one of the new members. "Isn't this exciting? Thirty Eco-kids. Wow!"

"I've never been in a club before," answered Kristin, grinning. "It feels totally cool."

Blond Vivian Rosenblatt nodded. "I had never been in a club before either. I just moved to Jewel Beach last year, and didn't have any friends yet. Now I've got lots!"

Sienna smiled. As an only child, she didn't mind the lack of brothers or sisters, but who could do without friends? She loved having people around her. And being part of the Eco-kids was especially fun. The constant chatter and movement, the buzz of energy. It was like an electric current.

People on the beach watched the Eco-kids amble by. Sienna realized that her club probably looked like a bunch of kids on a school field trip.

"This is embarrassing," Jess muttered. Behind her glasses, her dark eyes turned downward to her shoes. "Everyone's staring."

"Maybe they think we're a gang." Ramon made a mean face at a couple of teenage girls on a beach blanket.

"Cut it out." Cary poked him in the ribs. "You're just drawing more attention to us."

"Attention is a *positive* thing," Sienna pointed out. "Actually, this is a fabulous PR opportunity."

"What's that? Penguins rule?" Ramon pointed his toes outward, flattened his arms to his sides, and waddled.

His performance drew giggles from the Eco-juniors, the half dozen younger kids who always tagged along. They imitated Ramon's penguin walk.

Then Derek piped up with, "No, PR stands for puny rations, which is what I'm getting right now. Let's hurry it up, okay?" He jogged in tight laps around Ramon and the Eco-juniors.

Sienna rolled her eyes. Another hyper guy. With him, Ramon, and the little kids around, no wonder the group emitted high voltage.

"What PR stands for," she informed them, "is public relations. That's my specialty, you know." The club had appointed her official PR chief. It was her job to drum up other people's interest in the Eco-kids and their projects.

4

"What should we do, Sienna?" asked red-haired Webb Marsh. "Chant slogans?"

"How about, 'give a hoot, don't pollute'?" Eco-junior Gina Chang suggested.

"Or 'be aware, dare to care!' " added her friend Patti Pelligrini.

"How lame," Nate muttered.

"It'll be fun." Sienna clapped her hands. "Let's sing it out. Ready?"

"Let's not," Jess interrupted firmly. Her small glasses and the black braids crisscrossing over the top of her head made her look like a schoolmarm.

"Always the life of the party, aren't you, Jess?" Ramon waddled up to her penguin-style.

"Thank you." Jess bared her teeth at him.

Ramon shrugged. "Gotta admit, kids. Major geeky to walk down the beach singing stuff like that."

"That didn't stop you at the Can Do dance last fall," Webb pointed out. "Heard you did plenty of singing there. And dancing."

Sienna smiled. The Can Do dance in December really had been a blast. Plus, just as she had planned, it had also done a good job of getting other students at Jewel Beach Junior High interested in the school recycling program. The price of admission had been ten aluminum cans or five cans and one dollar.

"Well, that was a *dance*," said Ramon. "This is the *beach*."

"So? People dance at the beach all the time. And sing, too," Sienna told him.

"Not me." Ramon shook his head.

"Aw, come on," called Nate. "I dare you, Sanchez. Do the 'Recycle Rap.' Strut your stuff."

"Strut your own stuff," Ramon shot back.

Sienna planted her hands on her hips. "All right. If nobody else has the guts, I do." She cleared her throat. "The 'Recycle Rap'! Remember this one? Come on, let's sing it!"

Out of the corner of her eye she saw Derek and a couple of the other boys snickering at her. The Eco-junior boys laughed right out loud. Jess just stared at her shoes.

"The toe bone's connected with the . . . foot bone." Sienna clapped her hands with the beat. "And the rain-drop's connected with the . . . river."

Cary joined in clapping, and Kristin and Vivian started singing along. "The river's connected with the . . . ocean . . ."

A few of the other kids came in, too. The girl Eco-juniors even added a little hip-hop dance in time to the music. Sienna picked up on their moves, slipping in a few of her own. Then, even Ramon caved in and did a couple of his floor spins on the sand.

What a thrill to get people revved up! Sienna loved drawing them out of their shells and into some *action*. Being bored had to be the worst thing on earth. She leaped into the air for a ballet-style twirl.

Soon the whole Eco-kids mob followed behind her, most of them singing along with the "Recycle Rap" and some dancing. Front and center, she led them down the beach. The blue winter sky, the tossing ocean, the golden hues of China Hill up ahead all lifted her spirits even higher.

Everyone on the beach turned to watch the parade of Eco-kids go by. Two white-haired women in jogging suits waved. A father and his kids clapped in time with the beat. Some Japanese tourists pointed their camcorders.

Sienna smiled wide for them. She leaped and twirled again, all the while moving toward the path that led from the beach up to the China Hill picnic meadow.

This was all so perfect. She couldn't believe she had been bored just a few minutes ago. It was what she had always dreamed—the Eco-kids making themselves famous, spreading the word about saving the earth from poisons and pollution, changing minds everywhere. . . . All with Sienna Sabo at center stage!

For the dramatic finale of her dance, she planned to leap backward and fly into a scissors split. The second she leaped, though, she heard Jess and Cary call her name, and before she could do any flying or scissoring she whacked straight into something that sent her sprawling onto her rear end into the sand.

The first thing Sienna saw when she got over the shock was Ramon slapping his knee and laughing at her. She glared in his direction, then followed everyone else's gaze to what she had run into.

" 'WARNING,' " Jess read aloud. " 'NO TRESPASSING.' "

Sienna turned to find a blue sign with big white letters blocking off the China Hill path.

"Where did *that* come from?" she asked, rubbing her hip.

Cary helped her up and shrugged. "Never seen it before."

While Sienna dusted herself off, Jess read the rest

7

of the sign. " 'MORELAND AND MORTIMER DEVELOPMENT CORPORATION. FOR INFORMATION, PHONE 555-2BUY.' "

"Development corporation?" Freedom repeated.

"Development of what?" asked Vivian.

"Housing," replied Webb, "I'll bet."

Cary's black eyes squinted at the sign. "Housing?"

Webb waved up at the China Hill bluff above them. "Homes, condos, town houses, whatever. There's a shortage of them in this area. Pacific Beach, La Jolla, Jewel Beach . . . all the towns and neighborhoods around here are popular places to live. My parents' real estate agency in La Jolla is always on the lookout for property coming up for sale."

"Wait a minute." Ramon stopped laughing. "You mean somebody's going to build stuff on China Hill?"

"Looks like the Moreland and Mortimer Development Corporation is planning on it," Webb confirmed.

"You're kidding!" Cary shook her head.

Webb sighed. "Wish I was. My parents would know for sure, though. I could call them."

"But that company can't put buildings on China Hill," said Hallie. "It's so beautiful here."

Sienna nodded, sighing. The bluff really was a wonderful place. Beyond the No Trespassing sign, she knew, the trail meandered up through boulders and brush toward a little meadow near the top. Sienna always loved the tangy smell of the sage and grasses, the sounds of the sea below, and the twitters and chirps of birds.

"It's got awesome views from up there," Nate was saying. "Clear down to Mexico. They used to say you could see to China from the meadow. Which is how it got the name."

8

"Best spot around for whale watching," added Kristin. "Plus it's right on the beach."

"All of which adds up to why it's prime real estate." Webb pointed out. "Great place to visit, great place to live."

Still rubbing her hip, Sienna pointed an accusing finger at the sign. "They can't do that, can they? Everyone comes up here. It's practically a public park."

"Are you kidding?" Freedom Sutter snorted. "They can do anything they want. Developers are always taking over wild lands."

With his long blond hair and beaded headband, Freedom didn't just look like a radical. Sienna decided he sounded like one, too.

"They can't do *anything* they want," Jess countered. "There are laws that protect some areas. Environmental protection laws. You have to get permits to build things these days."

"But they've already got the sign up," said Hallie. "Doesn't that mean they've got their permit?"

Jess shrugged. "I don't know how it works."

"We could find out, though, couldn't we?" asked Cary. "Call somebody? Webb's parents? The government?"

"And then what?" asked Derek. "What can we do about it either way?"

Little Gina Chang popped up from behind Ramon. "Hey, we're the Eco-kids and Eco-juniors! It's our *job* to do something about it!"

Her friend Patti Pelligrini and the rest of the Eco-juniors rallied around her.

9

"That's right," Cary's little brother, Luke, pitched in. "It's our job."

The other Eco-junior boys, Luke's pals Matt Parker and Sam Fong, raised their fists. "Chi-na Hill! Save it now! Chi-na Hill! Save it now!" They tried to climb over the blue sign.

Ramon caught their sleeves and yanked them off it. "Wa-a-a-ait a minute, fellas."

"Why should we wait?" Freedom took a step forward as if to lead the charge. "I think the kids have the right idea. Ignore this stupid sign. Show the development corporation we won't give up China Hill." He raised his fist high.

Cary shook her head. "It would be against the law to go past this sign, Freedom. It says No Trespassing."

"Besides, there are other things we could do instead," Webb pointed out.

"Yeah, like our picnic, for instance," said Derek. "We could start with that." He nosed around in Hallie's backpack, which carried a bag of cookies her father had baked for them.

Hallie slapped him away. "Could we hold some kind of protest or something?" she asked Webb.

"Maybe," he answered, "but the first thing we should do is find out for sure what's going on."

"Fine." Ramon nodded enthusiastically. "Later you can ask your parents, Webb. Later we'll call the environmental protection people and all that. But for now let's have the picnic."

"Yeah!" agreed Derek. "The beach is a great place for a picnic. Right here." He dropped his backpack on the sand and tried to get at Hallie's again.

10

While the two of them struggled, the discussion went on. Freedom felt the Eco-kids should not let the development company win the first round on China Hill—that they should march straight up the path and picnic in the meadow, as planned. Cary felt they should skip the picnic, go back to the headquarters, and start making calls. Nate wanted to knock the sign over. Matt and Sam wanted to knock the sign over and paint graffiti on it.

Just as Matt aimed a rock at the sign, Sienna realized the tourists were still watching—and filming.

"Stop!" she shrieked, grabbing the little boy's arm and smiling big for the cameras. "Hah-hah! He's only joking!" she called loudly.

The tourists nodded and waved.

"This," Sienna hissed through her teeth, "is *not* good public relations, people."

Matt dropped his rock, but the heated discussion continued even after they all agreed to follow Ramon's suggestion to eat. They spread their towels and blanket right there beneath the No Trespassing sign, and brought out their sandwiches.

At least that made Ramon and Derek happy.

After the picnic, no one seemed happy.

At the Eco-kids headquarters in Cary's garage, the members gathered around a battered old wooden table. There was only space for eight, so some of them sat *on* the table and the rest perched on crates, boxes, and other things nearby.

"I still don't think we should have cut the picnic short for this," said Ramon. "We've been planning it

11

for weeks. We could have called a meeting tomorrow or something instead to deal with the China Hill problem."

"I agree," said Sienna. "The whole idea today was to get together just for fun—for one day to do no club work." She sat in her favorite spot, an old beanbag chair the Eco-kids had found in the garage when they took it over last fall. She crossed her legs in a yoga position, stretching her spine, feeling her rib cage expand.

"Oh, come on, you guys," Cary countered. "We took a vote and this is what we decided to do—come back here to discuss the problem. Plus, we're already here."

"Right," added Jess.

Hallie, the chairperson for the semester, rapped her knuckles on the table for attention. "Hush up, everybody. Webb's back from the telephone. What did your mother say?" she asked him.

He plunked his long frame into a rickety armchair and sighed heavily. "What do you want first, the good news or the bad news?"

"You mean there is good news?" asked Vivian.

Webb nodded. "My mother says that Moreland and Mortimer is a pretty good company. 'Reputable,' she said. They're known for trying to preserve the natural setting their houses are built on. They even use that as a selling point."

"So they *are* going to build on China Hill?" asked Cary.

"That's the bad news." Webb nodded again. "Town houses. I called the Moreland and Mortimer number after I hung up with Mom. Twelve town houses, they

12

said. 'Spectacular ocean views, parklike setting, luxurious yet affordable.' "

"Twelve!" Nate howled. "On China Hill? It's not big enough. And it's practically all hillside. Where are they going to put twelve town houses?"

Freedom snorted. "Oh, you know how they build houses these days. They won't let something like a hill get in their way. They'll build anywhere."

Webb sighed. "That's true. Anyway, the agent at Moreland and Mortimer said he's excited about the development because the community needs more housing. And he said what my mother said—that they plan to preserve the natural beauty of China Hill."

"How can they do that if they're building stuff all over it?" wondered Kristin. "My aunt lives in a new housing development and there are no trees or even bushes in sight. They had to cut and trample everything, just to get the construction machines in."

"Construction always damages the natural setting," Jess agreed. "You can't put up a building without cutting and digging and bulldozing."

"What else did the guy say?" asked Cary.

Webb grinned. "Well, here's the really good part. He was going on and on about how great these houses will be and all of the sudden he seemed to realize that I was a kid, and he asked me why I was calling."

"Did you tell him?" Vivian's eyes went wide.

Webb nodded. "I said I was a member of the Eco-kids and we're concerned about China Hill."

"Oh, great." Freedom shook his head. "Now you've blown our cover. We can't make a surprise attack."

"Maybe. But just listen." Webb sat forward. "He

13

says that his company plans to keep China Hill open to the community. We can still picnic there.''

"What about that No Trespassing sign?" asked Sienna. The bruise on her hip kept the sign vivid in her memory.

Webb shrugged. "All I know is he said they'll make part of the meadow into a public park. And he offered to send us the plans for the development so we can see it all on paper."

"*Part* of the meadow?" Jess frowned. "That would be a pretty tiny public park."

"Sure would," said Hallie. "Just a scrap."

"Well, at least they're trying," said Sienna.

"Trying?" fumed Freedom. "Trying to destroy the planet!"

Sienna rolled her eyes. "It's just one meadow, Freedom, not the whole world."

"Give 'em an inch and they'll take twenty-five thousand miles," said Ramon.

Jess smiled. "Clever. The circumference of the earth."

"But everybody's telling us they're a good company, right?" Sienna persisted. "They're going to provide a public park. Maybe it'll be really nice. They'll clear out the weeds, the snakes. . . ."

Cary frowned. "I've never seen a snake there."

"You never know." Sienna didn't understand all the fuss. She loved China Hill as much as anyone else, but a few town houses didn't seem like such a big deal.

She started to say so, but the appearance of a slender, dark-haired, very handsome young man in the Chens' garage made her freeze. Then her heartbeat sped up, her

14

mouth went dry, and her palms got sweaty. Those amazing things happened to her every time she saw Buck Chen.

She took a deep breath and let it out slowly. Why did Cary have to have such an awesome teenage brother?

Walking through the garage toward his old car in the driveway, Buck didn't even glance at Sienna or the other Eco-kids. He wore headphones and held a Walkman. He took about as much notice of her as of a speck of dust.

Sienna shut her eyes and focused on her breathing. In the positive imaging class, they said that when you wanted something, the best way to get it was to clear your mind and be open to possibilities. That allowed the right energies to flow and bring you the things you needed.

When she opened her eyes and tuned back in, Buck's car was sputtering away down the street. She sighed. Oh, well, maybe the things you wanted weren't supposed to come to you right away.

Loud voices pulled her back to the Eco-kids meeting.

"Let's go knock that sign down!" Nate kept insisting. "Show them right away that we're serious."

"Yes, and show them right away that we're lawbreakers, too." Jess shook her head. "I don't think so."

"Can I offer something here?" Sienna asked. "It's hard for me to get worked up about this China Hill thing. What Moreland and Mortimer told Webb doesn't sound so bad. They'll be careful with the plants and rocks and whatever. They'll let us hang out in the park. And how much can it hurt China Hill to have some houses on it?"

15

The room went silent. Pleased that people were finally paying attention to her, Sienna went on. "You know, it's important to keep everything in balance. In harmony. When we hear about something like a change on China Hill, we shouldn't immediately assume that change is bad. We shouldn't turn the development company into the enemy. Maybe there's a reason for China Hill to have town houses on it. Let's think about this."

She smiled, satisfied to have made her point. Glancing around the room, she found all eyes on her. Then she realized that few of the eyes looked friendly. In fact, many seemed to be shooting darts—at *her*.

2

"Sienna, are you nuts?" asked Cary.

"It *won't hurt* China Hill?" Freedom repeated.

Jess jumped in next. "If I hear one more word about perfect harmony—"

"I never said *perfect* harmony," Sienna defended herself. "I said harmony. Trying to work together. You know, peace and everything. That's important. Human relationships are just as important as helping the environment. We should all try to work harmoniously with each other."

Everybody was still eyeing her as if she had proposed killing Bambi and Thumper and all their forest friends.

"No one disagrees with you on that," Webb said, "but we're dealing with a development company here. We have to face facts. Moreland and Mortimer is out to make money, not peace and harmony."

"Maybe they can do both," Sienna suggested meekly.

Ramon shook his head. "Dream on."

"Get your head out of the clouds, Sabo," Nate told her.

Sienna exhaled loudly, which seemed to be the only

17

noise she was allowed to make without being drummed down. Couldn't a person express a different opinion around here?

"Well, I agree with Sienna on one thing," Jess said.

Sienna nearly fell over. "You do?"

"First of all, I'm sorry I snapped at you about the harmony thing," Jess offered.

Sienna shrugged. "I'll live." She and Jess had gotten on each other's nerves from almost the minute they met on the sidewalk four years before, with Cary caught in the middle. Ideas like positive imaging drove practical Jess up the wall. And Jess's refusal to think about anything new made open-minded Sienna see red. Sometimes they were like two pieces of flint grating against each other, throwing off sparks. But what would life be without a few sparks? Boring. Being friends with Jess was anything but boring. Besides, when it came down to the important things, Jess really was a friend.

The two of them exchanged a smile before Jess went on. "You're right about needing to *try* to work with the company. Give them a chance to show us what they've got planned before we attack them."

"Waste of time," Freedom huffed.

Nate nodded. "I'm with you, Freedom. I say take down the sign and post ourselves all over the bluff when they start construction so that they can't do it."

"How about a protest?" suggested Ramon. "Like the one we held last summer to free the wild dolphins from Aquarius Marine Park."

"Yeah, a protest!" Gina shouted between mouthfuls of the popcorn the Eco-juniors were munching.

Kristin, feeding popcorn to Cary's dog Lucille, said,

18

"Wow! I've never been to a protest before. It would be so cool!"

Jess frowned. "You make it sound like a party."

"Which it's not," Cary added. "Believe me. Not at all."

"Well, actually, a protest can have sort of a party atmosphere," said Sienna. "You know, everybody hanging out together? I had fun at the Aquarius protest."

"Right," said Jess, "just tons of fun. Standing around holding signs in front of Aquarius Marine Park. People staring at us like we're lunatics. Right."

Cary nodded. "Yeah, like when the security guards showed up. And threatened us. And tried to make us leave. Never had so much fun."

"Aw, what wimps." Ramon waved them off. "Hey, we survived, didn't we? A little protest at China Hill won't hurt you."

"I think we should get those building plans from Moreland and Mortimer first," said Vivian, "so that we'll at least know what we're protesting about."

Webb agreed. "It seems useless to march out there and rant and rave before we find out what's really going on."

"What's to find out?" Freedom demanded. "We already know they're planning to build up there. What more do we need? Let's just go." He stood up. "Who's coming with me?"

"Oh, sit down, Freedom," Hallie told him. "No one's going anywhere till we've taken a vote."

He sat down, but then a real debate got going. It seemed to Sienna there were five opinions for every

19

person in the room. They all argued back and forth. Even those who seemed to agree with each other turned out to have completely different notions on what to do. Other people changed their minds from one minute to the next. A couple of times she tried to say something and got drowned out. That was when she decided to do her yoga exercises instead. She twined her legs together in a lotus position, imagining the top of her head touching the sky, which automatically pulled and stretched her spine. Right away she felt mellow and relaxed.

The voices of the Eco-kids became a distant drone.

"Can't hear you, Sienna!" the drama teacher yelled from the rear of the auditorium. "Come on, *project* that voice. Remember you're playing for the back of the house."

"Yes, Ms. Tartoff!" Sienna yelled back.

She had the stage all to herself. She was Daffodil, Queen of the Flowers. It was her scene in the spring song and dance recital. She was supposed to be whispering to the trees and grasses. But of course it couldn't couldn't really be a whisper, because then the audience couldn't hear her. So it had to sound like a whisper that you could hear twenty yards away.

She made her voice louder but raspier. "There's something in the air. It's spring!"

"Much better." Ms. Tartoff nodded. "Now let's see the blossoming sequence. James, turn the tape on, please."

Sienna glowed with pleasure. A "much better" from Ms. Tartoff amounted to a "fabulous!" from anyone else. Now if she could get through the dance routine.

Just last week Ms. Tartoff had helped her choreograph it to a piece of classical music.

Moving into the first ballet position, Sienna took a breath to steady herself. Legs together, arms at her sides, she began to fold it all in—her knees bent, her arms tucked across her chest, head down.

"Smaller, smaller!" Ms. Tartoff directed.

The music started. A violin's high, thin voice. A single horn blowing.

Slowly, Sienna eased her shoulders back, raised one arm, then the other, unfurling herself like a blossoming flower. Standing tall, she swayed back and forth in the wind. Her arms curved toward the sun. Her face soaked up its rays. Imagining her feet as roots, she kept them planted firmly in one spot. That was the tricky part, because next came a pirouette, a twirl where she had to stay exactly in the same place while making two complete and graceful turns. It was supposed to look like a flower plucking itself from the ground. Finally came a leap across the stage—the flower's first step of freedom.

"All right," said Ms. Tartoff from just below the stage. "That's it."

Panting, Sienna looked down at her. "How'd I do?"

"Fine." Ms. Tartoff was studying her clipboard. "Benjamin, let's hear your pieces."

Before leaving the stage, Sienna allowed herself a moment to soak it all in. "Fine" meant "excellent." Her friend Mandy Sykes gave her a wink from the second row. Beyond Mandy were the rows and rows of seats that in another few weeks would be filled with an audience. A background set and props and lights would

21

transform the Jewel Beach Junior High auditorium into a Broadway theater and turn her into a star.

Well, a star for a couple of minutes, anyway. A star for one line and a short dance routine. The real stars would be Kendra Johnson, who was dancing to a piece by Claude Debussy called "Afternoon of a Faun," and Benjamin Medina singing a medley of Broadway tunes about springtime.

Still, a line was a line and a dance was a dance. Sienna beamed in rapture.

"*Ahem.*" Benjamin stood next to her, clearing his throat. "*My* turn?"

"Oh!" Sienna giggled. "Sorry!" She hurried off the stage.

Mandy whispered, "You were good!"

Sienna slid into a seat next to her.

A few seats away, Kendra gave Sienna the thumbs-up sign.

The drama group was so wonderful! Being onstage, honing her skills, hanging around with new friends . . . much more fun than her dance lessons with Madame de Fournier every Friday. And *very* different from an Eco-kids meeting. After all that arguing Saturday they had ended up voting on a compromise. They would not pull down the No Trespassing sign, but would wait till the building plans came and maybe hold a protest later.

Sienna leaned over to Mandy. "When do you do your scene?"

"James is after Benjamin and then I'm after him. Does my hair look okay?"

"Perfect." Sienna smiled. "As usual."

Mandy always looked great. Her hair made a blond

22

halo around her face. She had dewy pink skin, a button nose, and straight white teeth. Plus clothes. Lots of them.

What Sienna wouldn't have given for a closet like Mandy's. The Sykes family lived on the rich end of Opal Street, near the beach, and Sienna loved to go over there just to feel like a kid in a candy store. Skirts, blouses, pants, leggings, dresses, jeans, overalls, shorts, and shoes. Plenty of shoes. Imagine waking up every morning and pulling together anything you wanted for an outfit.

That very morning, for instance, Sienna hadn't been able to find anything in her own closet to go with her blue madras skirt. The first two blouses had looked okay, but somehow didn't feel right. Her body was a blank canvas, and her clothes were the colors and shapes. A true artist couldn't slap just any old paint on her creation. It had to *mean* something.

After rehearsal, she walked out with Mandy and Kendra toward the parking lot.

"Sienna!" Ms. Tartoff called after her. "Would you still like to put on the skits about recycling for your environment club?"

"Absolutely." Sienna hurried back to the teacher.

"Good. When you asked me about it last semester I suggested we wait until after the Christmas show and the holidays. Things have settled down a bit now." Ms. Tartoff took off her black-rimmed glasses and cleaned them on her sleeve.

"We need all the publicity we can get to encourage people to recycle," Sienna told her. "I'm the Eco-kids'

23

publicity leader, and we're trying to get more participation in the school recycling program.''

"Fine, then let's not waste more time. Why don't you jot down some ideas on what you'd like to do and bring them to me.''

"Great! I will.''

Elated, Sienna trotted off to rejoin Kendra and Mandy.

"Sounds like fun,'' said Kendra. Her hair fell in dozens of braids around her pretty brown face. "Do I get a part?''

"Why not?'' Sienna tried to sound casual. Kendra, asking her for a role in the recycling skits? An eighth-grader *and* one of the most popular people in the whole school! Sienna couldn't stay casual about it for long. "That would be awesome, Kendra. Jewel Beach Junior High's top actress appearing in a benefit performance for the Eco-kids!''

The three girls giggled.

"Can I be in it, too?'' begged Mandy.

Sienna felt as important as a Hollywood casting director. *"Hmm.''* She decided to tease her friend. "I'll think about it, Sykes. Are you truly committed to the Eco-kids cause? You were once heard saying you didn't believe in animal and environmental stuff.'' That was exactly what Mandy had said one day when Sienna had invited her to an Eco-kids meeting.

"I did not!'' Mandy defended herself. "I just don't like it when people panic about things.''

Sienna remembered the last Eco-kids meeting, where Freedom ranted and railed against Moreland and Mortimer and people clamored for a protest. "Well, you can have a spot in the show, anyway, Mandy, okay? Oh, there's my mom. See you guys tomorrow!''

They waved good-bye as she climbed into her mother's car.

''Hi, Mom! Oh, how I *love* the drama club!'' Sienna sighed and leaned the seat all the way back. ''It's so exciting! Even when I'm scared stiff.''

''You had stage fright during rehearsal today?'' Mom glanced at her across the front seat.

''Are you kidding? I always get stage fright! But then I get this incredible rush. You know, where suddenly your energy kicks in and you know you're in exactly the right place at the right time . . .''

Mom smiled. ''No, I don't know. I never in my life got a rush from being onstage. Exactly the opposite always happened. In fifth grade during a Halloween show I was supposed to play a trick-or-treater. That's all I had to say—'knock, knock, trick or treat.' But first I froze and then I cried and then I ran offstage.''

Sienna laughed. ''Oh, no. You're not a very good role model.''

''No, I'm certainly not, am I? But I don't think you need one, darling. You're a natural. You're very good onstage.''

''Thanks, Mom!'' Sienna beamed. ''You know, you *could* be an actress. You're so beautiful. They'd want you for all their movies.''

Her mother's rich auburn hair fell in a cascade of soft waves. Sienna's hair, though the same color, frizzed wildly every chance it got. Mom's skin was fair, flawless, and freckle-less. A mere glance at the sun brought

25

Sienna a dozen freckles, and one day without proper washing invited a whole guest list of zits.

"I wish I looked like you." Sienna popped down the passenger-side visor to frown at her face: a band of freckles over the nose, her hair completely out of control. At least she had interesting eyes. Big, greenish, expressive. "I hate my hair," she said.

"Sienna, you look very much like me."

"Oh, yeah, right. I look like you the way Little Orphan Annie looks like Michelle Pfeiffer."

"Darling, you're not going through a self-rejection phase, are you?" Mom reached over and twirled one of Sienna's curls around her finger. "You're a lovely girl."

Sienna smiled. "You really think so?"

Mom nodded. "I know so. Inside and out."

As they waited in freeway traffic on the way to Dad's shop in San Diego, they talked about the principles of self-rejection. Sienna had first heard about it in the Surviving Adolescence seminar she'd taken at the Institute of the Inner Self last year. Her parents were subscribers to the institute, where all kinds of experts got together to study human nature and give talks and classes.

"I don't think I'm really self-rejecting," she said. "I think I'm self-assessing."

"You're trying to discover your weak and strong points?" asked Mom.

Sienna nodded. "The seminar leader said that's a very common thing that preteens and teens do, more than any other age group. Supposedly when you're a younger kid you're not so aware of yourself, and when you're older you've got more confidence. But in the in-between years you're testing things. And that's why things that

people say to you hit you so hard. Like, when the seminar leader was a teenager other kids told him his head
was shaped like a buffalo's and he still remembers and
worries about it to this day.''

Mom glanced at her. ''Sienna, did someone say something to you?''

Sienna shrugged. ''Well . . .''

''What, darling?''

''Oh, it wasn't such a big deal.'' She tried to sound
nonchalant.

''Want to talk about it?''

Sienna sighed. ''Oh, I guess so. It wasn't like, really
awful or anything.'' She took a breath. ''Ramon said I
look like a palm tree.''

She saw her mother trying to restrain a grin.

''A palm tree?''

Sienna nodded. ''Last week at lunch. I haven't let
myself think about it much. I should have, though. It's
good that we're talking about it now, so that I won't
repress it anymore and let it become self-damaging.''

''It sounds like a compliment to me, Sienna. Palm
trees are beautiful. Tall, graceful, exotic . . .''

It always helped to talk problems over with Mom.
She made negatives seem positive. ''That's not what he
meant. He was being a jerk. He meant that I'm tall and
skinny and my hair sticks out. That kind of palm tree.''

''Did he say exactly that?''

Sienna shook her head. ''I know that's what he
meant, though.''

''But you're not going to internalize this comment,
are you,'' asked Mom, ''not let it stay with you?''

''Easier said than done. It's hard to just forget about

27

things like that. It kind of echoes in your head. I think of it whenever I look in the mirror.''

Mom nodded. ''I know. It's hard. A client once told me that the kitchen plan I designed for him seemed right for a family of rats—cluttered and crowded. He looked at my resume and saw Rhode Island School of Design and said, 'You sure that wasn't *Rodent* Island?' Now every time I look at my resume that's what I see. Rodent Island.''

Sienna couldn't help laughing. ''Oh, Mom. That's awful! What a jerk!''

''Exactly.'' Mom shrugged. ''It hurt at first, but now it's become funny. Which is one way of dealing with these things, I suppose—a sense of humor. What did they suggest in your seminar?''

''They said to let only those who *deserve* to have power over you have it. In other words, only accept criticism from people who deliver it with love.''

''Sounds good to me.'' Mom patted Sienna's hand.

A minute later they pulled up to the curb near Dad's shop. There was no parking lot, just whatever spots you could snag on the busy downtown street. Mom kept telling Dad he needed a more accessible location. Dad said that the customers who belonged in his shop would always find a way there.

Sienna hopped out of the car and opened the screened wooden door hung with a hand-carved sign, SABO ANTIQUES. Stepping into the tiny shop was like entering a different world. Her eyes adjusted from bright daylight to a darker, softer atmosphere. Her nose forgot smog and city streets and discovered the scents of old wood,

28

silk lampshades, and Persian rugs. By the swishing sound of a brush she found her father in the back room.

"Hi, Dad!" She ran up and kissed him. "Hey, you've got a smudge on your nose." She wiped it off with her sleeve.

Poor Dad. He always looked so sad. It was just his natural expression. Though handsome enough with thick gray hair, a strong nose, and a manly cleft in his chin, there was something in his deep blue eyes that made you want to reassure him.

The minute Mom walked into the room his face lit up. That always happened. She gave him a big hug and kiss. They adored each other.

"Oh, these are exquisite, Jon!" Mom spotted a pair of silver candelabra. "When did they come in?"

Dad put down his polishing brush. "Yesterday. They're the ones I bought at the auction in Pacific Palisades."

"Who are they for?"

"Don't know." Dad took off his smock and rolled down the sleeves of his shirt.

Together, he and Mom looked great: he, older and serious and distinguished-looking; she, young and beautiful and serene.

"You ordered them without a buyer in mind?" Now Mom didn't look so serene.

"Yes."

"I thought we agreed you wouldn't do that anymore," said Mom. "You would sell only your current stock unless you got a specific order from a customer."

"The candelabra will sell, Liv." Dad put away the credit card machine and locked the cash register.

29

Mom let out a long, loud sigh. "How do you know?"

"I know."

Sienna had heard this argument before. Mom was always trying to get Dad to run the business better. Because Mom was so pretty and an artist, people assumed that she was the dreamer and Dad was the practical one, but the opposite was true. Dad loved the history behind antiques and matching them up with the right people. The money part didn't interest him much.

"Yes," Mom said, "of course you know, Jon. As usual."

She turned and headed out of the shop, her heels colliding sharply with the wood floor. "Let's go home," she called over her shoulder, then let the screen door slam behind her.

"Sienna!"

At lunchtime Tuesday, Kendra and Mandy waved to her from across the cafeteria.

"Want to sit with us?" Kendra asked.

"Oh, wow. Um . . ." Sienna glanced around the table, which was occupied mostly by eighth-grade girls. Very popular eighth-grade girls. She and Mandy were the only seventh graders.

Several tables away sat Cary, Jess, Vivian, and some of the other Eco-kids. They hadn't spotted Sienna yet.

"Sure." She smiled, and Mandy made a space for her.

Sienna shrugged off a little nag of guilt. It wasn't written in stone that she had to sit with her old friends every single day, was it?

Kendra and Heather Connell were talking about a new store at the mall.

"It's gigantic!" claimed Heather. "The juniors department takes up the whole second floor."

"And they play great music videos," Tara Choi raved. "Have you been there yet, Sienna?"

She shook her head. "Not yet."

"Well, come with us next time. Maybe next Sunday?" Kendra proposed.

"That would be fun!" Sienna grinned. They liked her, a lowly seventh grader!

It had been weeks since she'd even been to the local mall. Cary and Jess were never interested in shopping. Cary's idea of an exciting outfit was a clean T-shirt and jeans with no dog hair on them. Jess had preselected sets of button-down shirts and pants to wear to school every single day, so that she wouldn't waste time deciding what to wear in the morning. It made Sienna shudder. Dressing, for her, was self-expression. It was creative. Important.

She and her mother used to go to the mall to see the new styles and colors and get ideas. Sometimes they'd buy blouses or scarves or a pair of earrings. They couldn't do that nowadays, though. Mom had said that until Dad's business picked up, they had to budget. Ulterior Designs, Mom's business, was doing great, but the money from that had to cover the family's expenses plus the ones for Dad's shop.

Which was probably why Mom had gotten so crabby with him last night. She had cooled off on the way home, and by dinnertime things had gotten back to normal. Thank goodness. Sienna hated it when they argued.

Tara tapped her arm. "I love what you're wearing, Sienna. You have the cutest clothes."

"Really? Thanks." She looked down at the silk-screened shift that one of Mom's artist friends had made for her birthday last May.

"That's why we first noticed you. Remember that outfit you wore the first week of school?" asked Kendra.

32

Sienna nodded. The red-and-white Western look. It had taken her an hour to put it together. Jess had gotten furious with her because they'd made it to class only a couple of minutes before the bell rang.

"You're a rebel," said Heather. "So creative, you do your own thing, but stylish, too. I could never pull it off. I never know what to wear with what."

"Oh, come on." Sienna laughed and looked at the girls sideways. "You're teasing me, right? You all have great clothes."

"*I'm* not teasing," Mandy assured her. "I think it's cool the way you think of things like that men's tie with the overalls you wore the other day. It looked really great."

Sienna smiled. "Well, thanks!" Finally someone appreciated her style. All she ever heard from Jess and Cary about it was teasing.

"*Ahem.*"

The sound of a clearing throat made her look up and find Freedom Sutter standing beside her. "Hi, Freedom. What's up?"

"Just want to make sure you know about the Save China Hill committee meeting tomorrow. Can you come?" He gave her a small smile.

"Well, no. I didn't join the committee. I'm kind of too busy." She noticed the girls had all stopped talking. "I'm already on the school recycling committee, the good ol' Jewel Beach Recycling Royals. Plus I'm on the pet care hot line every week. Matter of fact, I have my hot line shift tomorrow afternoon."

Freedom kept looking at her. "We need all the help we can get."

Heather whispered something to Kendra and they giggled, glancing up at Freedom.

Sienna wondered what they were whispering. "Well, maybe I can help another time."

Freedom gave a quick, sharp glance around the table. Probably, thought Sienna, he was observing what they ate for lunch. A strict vegetarian, Freedom had convinced Cary and some of the other Eco-kids to give up meat because it caused cruelty to animals. That didn't sound like a bad idea to Sienna. She wanted to give it a try. But she knew that she'd never act stuck-up about it the way Freedom did.

He walked away.

"He is so-o-o-o cute!" cooed Mandy the minute he left.

Sienna's eyebrows shot up. "Freedom? Cute?"

"Don't you love his hair?" asked Heather. "He's one guy who looks good in a ponytail."

"It's a mop," Sienna pointed out.

"He's got the perfect hippie look. Really sixties. The long hair, the sweet face, those tie-dyed shirts." Kendra squinted. "He should have a guitar and sing folk songs."

Mandy sighed. "He is so intense. Don't you think he's adorable?"

Sienna shrugged. "If you say so."

The girls talked about other boys—Oliver Camstock, cutest boy on the basketball team, Emilio Ochoa, best-looking boy in the whole school.

Many minutes later Heather asked, "What's that Save China Hill thing Freedom was talking about?"

"Yeah, I'll join if *he's* on it," warbled Mandy.

34

Sienna shook her head. "Bet you wouldn't. It's the kind of thing you said you don't like." She explained Moreland and Mortimer's plan to build town houses on China Hill and how the Eco-kids felt about it.

"Well, you've got to be careful about stuff like that," said Tara. "My uncle lost his job at a factory in San Francisco because some environmentalists said it was polluting the bay. They made the whole factory close down."

Kendra nodded. "Yeah, my dad says that's what these environmentalist kooks are doing. Forcing companies out of business 'cause of all the regulations they put on, and making people lose their jobs. People go into a panic about pollution, but things aren't really that bad."

"You think so?" asked Sienna. This sounded pretty different from Eco-kids' conversations, and she wasn't sure how she felt about it.

"I get so sick of those people protesting and yelling and screaming about things." Mandy wrinkled her nose. "It's like they just want to be the center of attention."

"They want to be trendy. It's hip to be into ecology now," Heather pointed out.

"Exactly." Tara nodded. "I don't think they mean half of what they say. They just want to get on the news."

Sienna didn't know how to answer. Should she mention that she herself had participated in an Eco-kids protest last summer—had even helped organize it? She and lots of her friends were environmentalists. That's what the Eco-kids was all about.

As if having read her mind, Kendra spoke up. "We're

35

not talking about *you*, Sienna. I mean, your group and the recycling program—that's great.''

"Right," agreed Mandy. "That's positive. It's the negative stuff I don't like.''

"Oh." Sienna nodded as if she understood but wasn't sure she did. This was something to think about.

"Yes, Mrs. Kiplinger. There are dozens of veterinarians who might be able to help you.'' Sienna cradled the phone against her shoulder and grabbed an envelope from a stack on the phone desk. "Just let me get your address and we'll send you a list of some vets who give low-cost services to senior citizens.''

"But I can't have just any vet for my little Bettina,'' the elderly woman replied. "You know Bettina. She's a very special sort of kitty.''

"Yes, she's very sweet. What breed is she again?'' Sienna asked, then put her palm over the receiver and hissed to the other Eco-kids in Cary's garage, "Could you keep it down? I'm on the hot line! ... Uh, yes, Mrs. Kiplinger, what did you say?''

"Alley!'' she shouted. "She's an alley cat. I found her in the alley behind my home, in fact, the same one that runs behind your condo building here on Opal Street.''

"Mmm-hmm," answered Sienna.

"My little Bettina has a sixth sense, I'll tell you. A marvel of a cat. She tells me before the phone rings, when the grocery boy is on the front path, and when we had that earthquake last year—''

"She predicted the earthquake?'' Sienna perked up, thinking what a helpful neighbor Bettina might be.

36

"No, but afterward the sweet thing would not leave my side. A dear little soul. Very protective, you know. Now you see why I need just the right doctor to help me look after her. I'm not very confident in the one we've been seeing, and he's so terribly expensive."

"I understand," Sienna reassured her. She pictured Mrs. Kiplinger's wispy white hair and faded blue eyes. "I'll send you this list, okay, Mrs. Kiplinger?"

"What list is that, dear?"

Patiently, Sienna explained it all again. She glanced at the clock. Four fifty-five. Only five more minutes on her shift.

Meanwhile, the volume of voices in the garage rose higher. It seemed that Freedom and Nate were still arguing against Jess and Webb about whether or not to hold a China Hill protest. Moreland and Mortimer had sent them the so-called building plans, which turned out to be nothing but a brochure with pictures of what the town houses would look like on the inside.

By the time Sienna finished the call with Mrs. Kiplinger, Freedom was holding up a sheet of paper that he and Nate wanted to glue over the company's sign. "WARNING," it read, "MORELAND AND MORTIMER KEEP OUT."

"That's not appropriate," said Jess.

"If I were Moreland and Mortimer that would make me really mad," agreed Cary.

Freedom shrugged. "So what if we make them mad? They haven't called us back. It's been an hour already since Hallie called them."

Webb shook his head. "They're not supposed to call us back today."

37

Hallie nodded. "I told them we wanted to ask them some questions and a secretary told me that the person we need to talk to is out of town. She took a message."

"I don't care what they told you," said Nate sourly. "We might as well try to talk to Santa Claus. They're just putting us off."

"Could be," Hallie agreed, "but let's give them till the end of the week."

Cary nodded. "We might as well. I'm still waiting for a call back from the mayor's office about whether or not Moreland and Mortimer has a permit to build on China Hill."

"And Webb is getting more info from his parents," Jess pointed out.

"I have a question," Sienna put in.

Freedom shot her a look. "I thought you didn't have time for this committee."

"I don't," Sienna admitted. "Does that mean I can't ask a question?"

"Go ahead," urged Hallie.

"What about the jobs issue?" Sienna asked.

Freedom eyed her. "Which jobs issue?"

Sienna thought for a minute. "Well, it's something I heard about the other day. Like, let's say we stop them from building on China Hill."

"Which we will," Nate insisted.

"Well, what if other groups stop them from building in other places?"

"Which they should if Moreland and Mortimer keeps trying to build in beautiful places like China Hill," said Cary.

38

Sienna nodded. "But eventually, what if they're not allowed to build *anywhere?*"

Freedom shrugged. "Who cares?"

"The people who work for the company might care," Sienna suggested. "I mean, if it puts them out of work."

"You mean you're sticking up for them?" Nate frowned.

Sienna prepared for another attack, like the one she got at the last meeting when she dared to voice her opinion.

To her surprise, Freedom spoke politely. "I see what you're saying, Sienna. But it's hard for me to worry about people who make their living wrecking the earth."

"I'm sure *they* don't see it that way," said Cary. "They probably see it as building homes, not as hurting the environment."

"That's true," added Webb. "That's how my parents see it, too. They think that town houses on China Hill are a great idea."

Sienna nodded. "It's not like everyone who works for Moreland and Mortimer is evil, you know. We've got to keep this in perspective."

"Why are you always defending them?" asked Freedom, back in his righteous tone again.

Sienna's back stiffened. Nothing could get her hackles up so fast as that tone of voice. She arched an eyebrow. "Why are *you* so narrow-minded?"

"Why are *you* so ready to let them do whatever they want?" Freedom demanded. "Destroyers and polluters of our planet have been in control for decades, and look where it's gotten us!"

39

"At least I'm willing to listen to other points of view," she countered, "which is more than you can say."

His blue eyes fixed on her. She glared back. What a bully. Heaven forbid anyone should disagree with him. How could Mandy possibly think he was cute?

"All right, all right, you two." Hallie waved a sheet of paper in the air as a white flag. "Let's calm down and get back to work. The Eco-kids have already voted to try to save China Hill, so if you've got new ideas on the subject you should bring them up at the next meeting. Okay, Sienna?"

Still fuming, Sienna nodded. At times like these she completely agreed with Mandy and the other girls about hotheaded environmentalists. Freedom could be a real bother. In fact, he was still staring at her. Probably waiting for a chance to make some other snappy remark.

"My hot-line shift is over," she said primly, gathering her things. "I'm going home now."

They didn't seem terribly sorry to see her go. A shadow of disapproval followed her out of the garage. When she reached the driveway and peeked back at the Save China Hill committee, they were already bent together in thought again, plotting their strategy against Moreland and Mortimer.

And at that moment, while looking backward, Sienna slammed straight into Buck Chen.

"Oh!" she cried, dropping her school books.

Buck had come around the corner of the house, headphones on as usual, eyes shut, prancing to the music.

"Hey!" he grunted.

"S-sorry!" she squeaked. Only Buck Chen could make her stutter.

40

"You okay?" He was rubbing his chin where her forehead had whacked it.

Sienna was dazzled, befuddled, mesmerized . . . anything *but* okay. She nodded, drinking in the cedary scent of his aftershave.

"Well, watch where you're going next time, all right?" He readjusted his headphones, not even glancing at her.

Her heart thudded. Her love for him gathered up its wings like a dove, ready to fly out to him. He moved past her toward his car, stepping neatly over her books.

After a few seconds Sienna could breathe again. She picked up the books. Walking home, the pavement was a cloud. Her brain was a bowl of noodles. Maybe it was the blow to her forehead, she thought, but that wouldn't explain the surge of happiness in her chest.

She had touched Buck Chen!

"Hey, Sienna!"

A voice from somewhere above made her jump. Again, her books landed on the ground.

"How ya doin'?" Ramon's face loomed into view as he dropped from his perch in a tree.

"Fine, before I saw you!" Her heart thudded for an entirely different reason this time.

Ramon hurried to help her gather her books.

"Why did you scare me?" she demanded.

Ramon shrugged. "Just saying hi."

"Well, hi, then," Sienna huffed. "And 'bye."

She pushed past Ramon. Hadn't he left his childish pranks behind yet? She only barely registered the hurt look on his face. As quickly as possible, she wanted to go back to her dreamworld and relive that moment when Buck had practically held her in his arms.

"Fabulous," Sienna's mother whispered.

"Wow," Sienna agreed. Together with her father they stood on a flagstone patio overlooking a broad carpet of green almost too perfect to be grass. Tall palms swayed in the winter sunlight. Banks of flowers in brilliant reds and pinks contrasted with the deep blue of the ocean just beyond.

Dad nodded. "I'd heard it was a showplace, but I never imagined this. What a spot for a party."

"Well, it isn't really a party." Mom read from the program she held. " 'Fine antiques auctioned for the benefit of the California Heart Foundation, one of Rowena Pollard's favorite charities.' "

Sienna glanced at the house behind them, a modernistic mix of different angles and levels in steel and glass. Guests milled around the grounds and under a huge party tent striped in white and sea blue.

"Does Mrs. Pollard actually *live* here?" she asked.

Mom nodded. "She just had the house built. Tore down the old one. This is one of the most valuable pieces of property in La Jolla."

Sienna whistled. No one built houses like this in

Jewel Beach, the town just next door down the coast. Rowena Pollard could afford to. Her father had founded the Price Rite supermarket chain, which she inherited and now ran herself.

"The woman is a marvel," Dad said quietly. "Eighty-one years old, but about as agile as I am. When she came into the store and bought those Chinese chairs last summer, I couldn't believe who I was dealing with. Wait till you meet her."

"She must be something, to have the energy to bring this space into being." Mom nodded. "Imagine looking out at this view every day. A garden like this. A house like that."

"I'm not as fond of the house," said Dad, "as I am of the view." He dropped his voice lower. "In fact, the house is a monstrosity."

Mom frowned. "Oh, Jon, please. Do you realize who the architect was? Kendall Kirstner!"

"I don't care if the architect was Kendall Kirstner or Mickey Mouse. Awkward is awkward. Ugly is ugly."

Sienna saw her mother's cheeks flush pink.

"You're so traditional, Jon. If a building doesn't fit an established style, you . . ." Mom let the sentence die when a woman in a tuxedo appeared with a silver tray.

"Care for an hors d'oeuvre?" the server asked.

"Thank you." Mom nodded. She and Dad took little puffs of pastry filled with mushrooms.

"And for you, miss?" The woman bent toward Sienna.

She shook her head. "No thanks." After the server left she said, "I've already had some of those. I'm waiting for the caviar to come around again."

43

Dad smiled at her. "How many twelve-year-olds do you know who crave caviar?"

Sienna rolled her eyes. "Yes, Dad, I know. It's fish eggs. You've already told me a zillion times."

"A good reason not to take one's daughter to formal occasions, Liv. She develops expensive tastes." Dad winked.

The gourmet food was just one reason Sienna loved going to charity balls and auctions and gallery openings. Her parents got invited to them because of their work, and Sienna was only too happy to tag along. What a thrill, spotting celebrities and visiting mansions and fancy hotels. It felt like being on *Lifestyles of the Rich and Famous*. But her absolute favorite part was the clothes. Beautiful, beautiful clothes. Men in black tuxedoes with silk cummerbunds. Women in lamé and sequins and floating chiffon. Or for daytime and outdoor events like this one, the men wore light colors and the women came in sweeping flowered dresses or elegant suits.

Mom, as usual, broke the mold by mixing styles, pulling together a long, tropical print skirt with a brocade jacket in just the right shade of cream to set off her hair. Dad wore his pearl-gray suit and pink Italian tie. The two of them could have posed in a fashion magazine, they looked so perfect together. Gazing at her parents, Sienna sighed happily.

As for herself, she had worn her green velvet vest over an ankle-length, slim green dress that she and Mom had found in a vintage clothing shop downtown. She added a yellow, crushed velvet cap, also from the vintage shop, and Mom's little pearl earrings.

44

Another server came by with the caviar tray, making her even happier. Into her mouth she popped a cracker dotted with dollops of chopped egg and gleaming black caviar.

"Oh, my. *Mmm,*" she mumbled between swallows.

Dad grinned, shaking his head.

"We should probably join the crowd," suggested Mom. "We haven't been mingling."

Dad nodded. "We haven't even seen our hostess yet. What time does the auction start?"

"Three-thirty. But we're not here to buy, Jon, all right?" Mom reminded him. "The reserve price list is astronomical. Please don't fall in love with anything."

Dad took Mom's hand and kissed it. "Only you."

As they strolled toward the tent, Sienna recognized the mayor of San Diego, two different movie stars, and the weather woman from Channel Six.

"Don't stare, darling," Mom whispered.

"I can't help it," Sienna whispered back. "That's Alicia Adelante! She's in that new sci-fi show on TV. Look at her outfit!"

Mom took a quick, discreet peek at the actress's frilly white poet shirt and flouncy red skirt.

"Can I get her autograph?" Sienna begged.

"In a minute," Dad answered. "Here's Mrs. Pollard."

"Well, Jonathan Sabo, hello!" The older woman smiled at Dad. Her hair, pure white, was swept away from her face into a braided knot behind one ear. She wore a blue silk dress, a single string of pearls, and no makeup.

Though small, Mrs. Pollard was no "little old lady,"

Sienna quickly realized. There was something very bright about her, and tough, too.

Her brown eyes swept over Sienna and her mother. "I see you're escorting two beautiful ladies today, Jon."

Mom smiled. "Thank you."

"This is my wife, Liv Engstrom," said Dad, "and our daughter, Sienna."

"Sienna. What a lovely name! A pleasure to meet you both. I'm so glad you came. Have you had something to eat yet? A drink?"

"The hors d'oeuvres are wonderful," Sienna answered.

Mrs. Pollard laughed and focused on her. "What a treasure you are." She took Sienna's hand. "So poised. And a true beauty. My congratulations to you, Liv and Jon."

Sienna basked in the praise.

"Arthur!" Mrs. Pollard pinched the sleeve of an old man walking by.

He wore suspenders over a blue shirt and was biting into an apricot half filled with creamy cheese. Sienna made a mental note to try one later.

"Arthur, let me introduce you to someone you should know."

The man swallowed quickly and wiped his hands on his napkin.

"Jonathan Sabo and Liv Engstrom, and their charming daughter, Sienna . . . Which last name did they give you, dear?" Mrs. Pollard asked.

"Both. Engstrom-Sabo. But I use Sabo because it sounds the best."

"Sienna Sabo." The older woman smiled. "This is

46

Arthur Kingston. He lives on Diamond Court in Jewel Beach. Arthur is a former neighbor of mine.''

Mr. Kingston smiled and extended his hand, muttering how do you dos.

''Arthur is in dire need of having that house redone, I keep telling him. I hope that one day he'll believe me and go straight to your shop, Jonathan, for the furniture.''

''Thank you,'' Dad answered, stuffing his hands in his pockets.

''What style is your home, Mr. Kingston?'' asked Mom.

Shrugging, the man looked blank.

''Oh, Arthur would have no idea.'' Mrs. Pollard laughed. ''But it's Mediterranean architecture. Red tile roof and so forth.''

Mom nodded. ''I think I've seen it. We live not far from Diamond Court.''

Dad slipped his arm around Mom's waist. ''Liv owns a home-styling business.''

''It's called Ulterior Designs,'' Sienna piped up.

Mrs. Pollard smiled. ''How clever. You do interior decorating, Liv?''

''In a way,'' Mom replied. ''I'm an interiors artist. I help my clients envision what 'home' truly means to them and bring it to reality. I use some of my own works—weavings, paintings, custom upholsteries—as well as furniture from Jon's store and whatever else seems right.''

''Fascinating.'' Mrs. Pollard nodded. She swept a hand toward her new house. ''Ronald Beekman did my interiors. But I can't say I'm at home here.''

47

Sienna tried to look interested. Once people found out about Mom's work they went on forever about their houses. She glanced around the tent, and spotted Alicia Adelante autographing a cocktail napkin for a short man with frizzy hair.

"You only just moved in, didn't you?" Mom was saying to Mrs. Pollard.

"Yes, but . . ." The older woman squinted thoughtfully at Mom. "Why don't you call me some time soon, dear? I'd like very much to hear your ideas about the house. Jonathan, you have my phone number, don't you?"

Sienna noticed that Mr. Kingston, who had apparently grown bored with the conversation, too, was staring at her. She turned and smiled back.

He rubbed his chin. "You look familiar, young lady. Are you an actress, maybe?"

Sienna was delighted. "Well, actually, I am, but—"

"Aha! That's where I've seen you. On the TV."

Mrs. Pollard shook her head. "Good gracious, is that right? The girl is not only beautiful and bright but talented, too?"

Sienna looked at her parents. "Well, thank you, but . . ."

"Sienna appears in school plays," Dad explained, "but I don't believe she's been on television yet."

"Oh, yes she has," Mr. Kingston insisted. "I saw her. Couple times. I know! It was a show about those kids in Jewel Beach. The E—E-something . . ."

"Oh!" Sienna brightened. "The Eco-kids!"

Mom laughed. "Of course. You must have seen her on the television news. I'd forgotten. Sienna was on Channel Six twice with her group."

"The Eco-kids?" asked Mrs. Pollard. "Is that a club, dear?"

Sienna nodded. "We do things to help animals and the environment."

"That they do," agreed Mr. Kingston. "Some of your buddies came to talk to me about my girl Gem last summer."

"That's his dog," explained Mrs. Pollard, "on whom he simply dotes."

"Oh!" Sienna cried. "You're *that* Mr. Kingston? Gem's owner? Cary told us all about—" She interrupted herself, realizing she probably shouldn't say what she was about to say.

"Yep." He chuckled. "Your friends came and told me not to let Gem run loose and so on. I admit. That was me. And those kids were right, you know. Now I keep my girl inside with me. Got her fixed not to make more puppies, too. She was a real rascal before. Made lots of pups, and I didn't know what to do with 'em."

"You gave three of them to us," Sienna reminded him. Actually, he had left them in a box on Cary's doorstep. Luckily, Cary's mom let her keep one, Ramon took another, and Cary's dad found a good home for the third.

"How interesting," said Mrs. Pollard. "Tell me, Sienna, what sorts of projects does your club undertake?"

Sienna explained how they had helped a marine mammal rescue group free two wild dolphins from an amusement park, and how they had started the pet care hot line and the school and neighborhood recycling projects. She ended with the Save China Hill committee.

Mr. Kingston's eyes widened. "You're kidding!" he

49

almost shouted. "You mean somebody's trying to build on the bluff? They're crazy!"

"That's what some people in the Eco-kids believe, because—"

Mr. Kingston interrupted her. "My house is on the street that runs along the top of that bluff. I'm half a block away from what you're talking about. They're not going to put houses up there!"

"They're not?" Sienna asked.

Mr. Kingston shook his head. "Nope. Sure aren't. 'Cause I won't let 'em."

"You won't?"

"No, ma'am. I take my Gem walking out there every day. Folks from the senior center stroll there to picnic, get their exercise. Couple of friends of mine are bird-watchers—they spot a lot of different kinds on China Hill. Why, I see all ages on that bluff, enjoying the view, passing the time. We've got few enough places left in this town to stretch the legs. They want to build on every little handkerchief-sized plot they find, don't they? *Hmph!* We'll see about this."

"Just what do you intend to do about it, Arthur?" asked Mrs. Pollard.

"Well, I don't know yet, Rowena, but I'll do something."

Mrs. Pollard gestured toward Sienna. "Maybe you should join forces with these young people."

"That would be great, Mr. Kingston. Would you like me to ask Cary to stop by and talk with you? She's on the Save China Hill committee."

"Well, it didn't hurt last time your friends stopped

50

by." The old man rubbed his chin. "All right. You do that."

Mrs. Pollard clapped her hands. "How exciting. A community effort getting organized here at my little garden party. Such a thrill to put the right people together. Now, you'll keep me posted on your progress, won't you? And, Liv, do give me a ring sometime. I'd love to hear your ideas on the house." With a rustle of silk, she moved away to greet the other guests.

That evening, Sienna sat on the living room rug reading and rereading the scribbled autographs she'd collected at Mrs. Pollard's.

"Look at this one!" she passed a blue cocktail napkin to her father.

Her cat, Number One, opened a golden eye to watch the napkin go by. He lay tummy-up in Sienna's lap, all four paws in the air, a silver, sleepy puff of fur.

Mom read over Dad's shoulder. " 'To Sienna Sabo, a bright young person with a big, bright future. I'll look for your name in lights. Best wishes, Alicia Adelante.' "

"I told her I'm going to be an actress," Sienna explained. "She was really encouraging."

"That's marvelous, darling." Mom smiled.

After the auction they had driven to historic Old Town in San Diego for Mexican food, then stopped at a French bakery on the way back for pastries to eat by the fire.

Sienna loved time at home with her parents. Mom had lived up to her claims for making houses into homes, or in this case, a condo into a home. The fire blazed in a flagstone hearth hung all over with colorful ceramic

51

masks Mom had made during college. The walls, painted peach, glowed in the firelight. Comfort was the living room's theme, Mom said. Through Dad's store she had found the extralong and wide sofa, perfect to stretch out on, and two oversized armchairs perfect to curl up in. Huge tasseled pillows made great nesting spots on the rug.

Dad handed back the autograph. "Did you get the mayor's?"

Sienna nodded and showed him another napkin. " 'Remember to vote.' And here's the one from Rod Raines, the actor in that new spy movie."

"Oh." Mom turned up her nose. "That horribly violent one."

"He didn't look too violent in person," Sienna reported. "He's much smaller than he looks on screen and he wears really thick glasses. Plus he had his mouth full of the duck pâté."

Dad laughed. "Sounds like you enjoyed yourself this afternoon."

Sienna nodded. "It was useful, too, 'cause I'm going to call Cary and tell her about Mr. Kingston's wanting to help save China Hill."

Mom leaned against Dad, stretching her long legs along the sofa's empty half. "Jon, speaking of usefulness, I appreciate your mentioning my work to Mrs. Pollard."

Dad shrugged. "Isn't that why we go to those things? To make contacts? Drum up business?" He winked at Sienna. "Other than to feed our daughter, of course."

Sienna poked him in the leg.

"You're doing it again." Mom frowned at him.

Dad's eyes snapped back to her. "Doing what?"

"Taking the focus off yourself. Hiding your light under a bushel. Scurrying out of the spotlight. Whatever you want to call it, it amounts to the same thing." Mom shook her head. "You did it at the auction. When Mrs. Pollard tried to hook you up for some business with Arthur Kingston, you immediately moved the conversation to *my* work. Do you even realize you're doing it?"

"Liv, don't invent problems." He sounded perturbed.

And with that, Mom got worse than perturbed. Her eyes flashed. "Now you're pretending it's all in my head, because you don't want to face the truth. Your business is failing, Jon. Face it. And *do* something about it."

Dad squinted. "You want me to be one of those slick salesmen. To go to those events and talk up my store like those other hucksters who show up. Well, that's not me. My store and the merchandise in it speak for themselves."

"Furniture," said Mom, "cannot talk. If people don't come and see it they'll never know what treasures you've gathered, Jon. You have such a talent for finding these wonderful things. Why do you refuse even to run an ad in the newspaper? What possible harm—"

Suddenly Dad stood up. Sienna jumped. All the action startled Number One. He bolted from her lap and ducked under the end table.

"This makes me furious, Liv." Dad's voice was ominously low. "Your doomsday predictions are counterproductive. Why do you do this? If you wanted a life of luxury you shouldn't have married me."

Sienna's heart stopped. In all her parents' arguments,

53

she had never heard either of them say anything so terrifying.

Mom glanced at her, face clouded with both tears and anger. "Excuse us, Sienna. I'm sorry we're subjecting you to this. We should continue our discussion in private, Jon, don't you think?"

Dad stomped off toward their study at the back of the condo.

After they'd gone, a soft, plaintive meow came from under the end table. Number One's beautiful eyes sought Sienna's.

"Come here, sweetheart," she mumbled, reaching out to him.

He stood up, shook himself, and padded cautiously back to her.

"It'll be all right," she assured him, scooping him up for a hug. "I think."

5

Holding up a brown dress, Kendra gazed into the Kaleidoscope Juniors shop mirror.

Tara wrinkled her nose. "I hate the lace. It looks like something my great-grandmother would wear."

"What do you think, Sienna?" asked Kendra.

Sienna leaned her head to the side. "Well, it is retro. But the color is great on you. Would you wear a hat?"

"A hat?" Kendra shrugged. "Should I?"

Sienna rummaged through a bin. "With this, you could make it into a great forties look." She handed Kendra a little cloche hat pinned with a silk violet.

"I'll go try them on." Kendra hurried to the fitting room.

"I'm glad you came with us, Sienna," said Mandy, flipping through a rack of sweaters. "It's like having our own personal fashion consultant."

"Yeah," agreed Tara. "I love those shoes you helped me find. I can't wait to try them on with . . . What was it you said?"

"The paisley leggings and the rust sweater."

Not to be confused with the purple jeans and white sweater Tara had also bought that day, thought Sienna,

55

or the baby-doll dress and high-top shoes. Sienna couldn't believe how much stuff Tara had gotten. Mandy wasn't far behind, and Kendra was catching up with them. It was like a contest. Who could put the biggest dent in their parents' credit card?

Sienna wasn't in the race. She didn't have a credit card. She had three dollars and ninety-two cents left over from her month's allowance. All she'd bought was a polka-dotted baseball cap on sale at the drugstore. Maybe she shouldn't even have gotten that. The way Mom talked last night, the Sabo-Engstrom family might be going broke.

She'd rather not think about her parents' argument. It had been very negative. Even after they'd gone to the study she'd still been able to hear them. Mom had said they could barely make the condo payment that month. They'd had to take money out of their savings to cover merchandise at Dad's store that he had thought would sell right away. If he didn't put both his feet on the ground, Mom said, they could lose everything they had.

Cancel, cancel, Sienna repeated in her thoughts. It was a positive imaging method she had learned in the seminar last fall at the Institute of the Inner Self. You could also say "erase, erase," if you wanted, or "blank, blank," or anything else, the idea being to prevent negativity from entering your way of thinking. Negativity was like a weed that could root and grow and take over, leaving no room for creative, constructive ideas.

Sienna wondered if her parents had been practicing the positive imaging method lately. It didn't seem like it. She had heard plenty of negativity flowing between them.

The method didn't help her much that day, either. As the afternoon wore on her energy fizzled. Memories of her parents' argument dragged her down. Not even her new friends' shopping enthusiasm helped. In fact, it was beginning to get to her. Like soldiers invading the mall, they left no store unshopped.

When Mandy found a pretty bracelet at the new department store, she seemed to want it more because it was something to buy than because it was something she loved. Sienna began to feel like she was watching a TV game show. *Win everything in the mall, just by flashing your credit card.* It was exhausting.

She was glad when Tara's mother came to pick them up.

" 'Bye, Sienna!'' her friends chorused when Mrs. Choi dropped her off at home. "We'll do this again sometime soon!"

"Sure, thanks," she called back, muttering to herself, "not too soon."

One thing that could cheer Sienna up was the drama club.

On a Monday afternoon she and five other members marched onto the auditorium stage in tight formation, two rows of three.

"Closer together," shouted Ms. Tartoff, "and walk in unison. Remember you are a six-pack of aluminum cans. You're very stiff, very formal. You do everything together."

Sienna drew herself up rigidly, standing as straight as she could. The six-pack halted at center stage. On

57

a cue from a helper offstage, they all turned to face the audience.

The can next to Sienna had the first line. "Gee, I hope somebody buys us," said James O'Connor.

"Yeah, everyone else is being bought," added Mandy, the can behind her.

They were supposed to be a six-pack of soda on a store shelf. It had started as Ramon's idea during a Recycling Royals brainstorming session. Mr. Montoya, a science teacher and the Eco-kids' faculty sponsor, helped them flesh it out. They came up with a title, "Break Out of the Pack." Sienna had taken that one and some other good ideas to Ms. Tartoff. With the drama club they had worked them into skits about recycling. The performance was scheduled for school assembly in a few weeks. They would do "Break Out of the Pack," "Second Chances," and "Down in the Dumps."

All the cans glanced up and down as if watching other six-packs being taken off other shelves. Sienna tried to keep her body straight, turning only her head up or down.

"Look, we're the only ones left!" cried the third can in her row, Tommy Kim.

The others frowned and worried.

"We are?"

"Oh, no!"

Then came Sienna's first line. "Well, but is it so bad to be different? Do we have to do what everyone else does?"

The other cans turned and stared at her.

"Of course we do!" they insisted.

Then one of them glanced up at the ceiling. "Look! Here comes somebody! He's going to buy us!"

They moved their shoulders up and stood on tiptoes as if someone were lifting the six-pack. Then they shuffled offstage backward.

"That's fine," called Ms. Tartoff. "Here's where the curtain falls. Now take your spots for act two."

Hurrying back out, Sienna reminded herself to breathe deeply. All her big lines came in this scene. Nervousness made her feet cold and her palms sweaty, but in the most delicious way. There was nothing that topped the thrill of being onstage, even for rehearsal.

She stood in the spot Ms. Tartoff had shown her near center stage. Mandy and Erin Manning-Bishop sat on the edge of the stage, legs dangling over. Tommy lay sprawled with his arms behind his head. In a corner James sat with his legs crossed, and on the opposite side Lita Yusef stood on her head.

Ms. Tartoff nodded. "Okay, curtain goes up here. Then count to ten, Mandy, and go."

After ten seconds, Mandy sighed loudly. "I feel empty."

"Me, too," echoed Tommy.

James nodded. "Hollow inside."

"Drained!" agreed Lita.

Mandy sighed again. "I think it's time for . . . you know."

"Already?" asked James.

Erin shrugged. "That's how it goes. The story of our lives."

Stepping forward, Sienna held up a hand. "Wait a

minute. This can't be all there is. There must be more to us. We can't just end up in the—"

"*Shh!*" the others hissed. "Don't say it!"

From the right side of the stage entered Benjamin, wearing heavy leather gloves and a cap he'd borrowed from Mr. Rinehart, the school custodian.

He walked slowly, pretending to haul a big bag. A few feet behind him came three other actors. They shuffled along as if being dragged in the bag.

"You are empty," Ms. Tartoff coached the new arrivals. "Empty and depressed. You are used-up soda cans, and you believe your lives are over."

The cans Benjamin "dragged" let their shoulders sag and their heads droop.

"Well, this is it," said James.

The six-pack cans shuffled toward the bag—all except Sienna.

She contorted her face and wrung her hands. "No! This can't be it! This can't be the end! I won't go. I won't!"

Then, from offstage, a voice . . . "That's right, soda can! You don't have to!"

Kendra ran onstage. The green bed sheet she wore for a cape sailed behind her.

"It's . . . it's Rita Recycle!" gasped Benjamin the custodian. He "dropped" the cans in surprise.

"That's me!" Kendra confirmed. "And it *doesn't* have to end this way! There is much more to you than this. You don't have to go to the—"

"*Shh!*" The cans hushed her, trembling. "Don't say it, please!"

Rita Recycle winked. "Well, the you-know-what. All you have to do is follow me!"

The cans "jumped" out of the custodian's trash bag, looking peppy and alive again.

Rita Recycle moved to center stage to say, "Don't be down in the dumps!"

Sienna stood beside her. "Right! Break out of the pack!"

Then the whole troupe joined in with, "*Recycle!*"

A burst of applause from the drama club audience followed them offstage.

In an excellent mood, Sienna showed up for hot-line duty at Cary's Wednesday afternoon, right on time. Crowded as usual, the Eco-kids headquarters held the Save China Hill committee plus a few Eco-juniors who were folding flyers with information about the new neighborhood recycling pickup hours.

Jess did a double take at her watch when she saw Sienna. "What? I don't believe this. It's a miracle."

Sienna ignored her, continuing to make her way through the garage toward the phone in the Chens' kitchen.

"Yeah," Cary chimed in. "It's only four o'clock, Sienna. Are you feeling okay? Let me get the thermometer. You must be sick or something. You're actually on time."

"Hah, hah. You two are a real comedy team, aren't you?" Sienna made a face.

But nothing could burst her bubble that week. She was riding high from the recycling skit rehearsals.

While pulling the Chens' telephone out from the

kitchen to the hot-line desk in the garage, Sienna thought over the rehearsal sessions. There had been only a few glitches. In one of the skits, "Second Chances," Tommy played a juvenile delinquent plastic drink bottle. One day he forgot some of his lines and his plastic bottle cap hat kept falling off. And during the other skit, "Down in the Dumps," where items of trash told sad stories about how they had ended up in the city dump, Ms. Tartoff said they would have to punch up the dialog because it was too depressing. But in the end she had told them things were going well, which translated to "Terrific!"

Sienna put the telephone on the hot-line desk and settled into the chair. She arranged all the things she needed—the big red information notebook, the envelopes, pen, notepad. For a while she listened to the Save China Hill meeting. Freedom was complaining that Moreland and Mortimer still hadn't called back.

"Did the mayor's office get back to you?" Hallie asked Cary.

Cary nodded. "Sort of. One of the mayor's assistants said they're still checking on whether or not Moreland and Mortimer has all the government permits they need to build on China Hill. They're supposed to call me again."

Sienna's thoughts drifted back to the skits and how great they were going to be in performance with costumes and a few props. By then they'd have the wrinkles ironed out, and—

The phone rang, startling her.

"Hello?" she answered. "I mean, pet care hot line. May I help you?"

"Pet care hot line?" replied a puzzled voice. "What's that?"

"Well, we give free information about pet care. Is that why you called, sir?"

"Are you the E—E—?"

"Eco-kids?" provided Sienna.

"That's who I'm looking for," the man answered. His voice sounded familiar. "I need to talk to the Eco-kids."

"Any particular one?" asked Sienna. "We're a club and—"

"I want to talk about what's going on out there on China Hill," he interrupted. "I met a young lady who said—"

This time Sienna interrupted him. "Oh, you must be Mr. Kingston!"

"That's right."

"I'm Sienna Sabo. It was me you met at Mrs. Pollard's auction."

"That's right. You said you kids are working against the building up there. What are you doing about it?"

"Well, I don't exactly know because I'm not on that committee, but they're all right here, so just a minute, okay?"

She put a hand over the phone receiver. "Excuse me, everybody."

The committee members looked her way.

"There's someone on the phone who wants to talk about China Hill. It's Arthur Kingston. You know, the guy on Diamond Court."

"Mr. Kingston?" repeated Cary.

"Gem's person?" added Cary's little brother, Luke.

He turned to the other Eco-juniors. "That's the one who owns my dog Bal's mother. Her name is Gem."

Cary walked to the phone. "How did he find out about—"

"I told him. I met him at an auction I went to with my parents a couple of weeks ago and somehow the subject came up, and he said he wanted to help us. I guess I forgot to tell you." Sienna shrugged.

"I guess you did."

Cary's tone made Sienna wince. She felt a little guilty about forgetting. At Mrs. Pollard's auction, she had promised Mr. Kingston that the Eco-kids would visit him to talk about saving China Hill. But with all that had been happening lately, the whole thing had slipped her mind.

"Wow," said Cary after hanging up with Mr. Kingston. "He is really upset about the building plan. He says he'll do whatever he can as a local homeowner to stop them." She grinned wide.

"That's great," said Webb. "Now we've got an adult in our corner."

"Hey, maybe that means there are others who feel the same way," suggested Nate. "Maybe we could get other neighbors to help. Everyone around here uses China Hill."

Cary nodded. "Mr. Kingston said he's going to talk to his neighbors in the Diamond Court Homeowners Association and also to people at the senior recreation center."

"I'm sure people on our street would want to help, too," Jess noted. "Penny Allbright and the Sobieskis are always interested in our projects."

"While you're at it," Sienna put in, "get them to

64

sign a petition. That always gets attention." She had resumed her spot at the hot line desk. "On the news reports they always talk about how many signatures a group got on their petition to do such and such."

Freedom perked up. "Yeah, if we get enough signatures, maybe that would prevent construction up there."

Webb shook his head. "I don't know about that. Legally, if the developer gets all the right permits from the government, I'm not sure local residents can stop them."

"Okay, let's start making a list of these ideas," said Hallie. *Find out about legal stuff,* she jotted down. *Talk to local neighbors, possibly circulate petition.*

Cary nodded. "I invited Mr. Kingston to attend the Eco-kids general meeting next Saturday so we can all fill him in on what we're doing. Maybe he can think of something."

Hallie added to the list, *Fill in Mr. Kingston.* She looked at Sienna. "It's really good that you made that contact for us, Sienna. Good work."

Sienna shrugged. "No problem. All I did was tell him about the Eco-kids and—"

"But next time," Cary broke in, "try to tell us about something like this sooner, okay? We could have gotten started on this last week if you had told us about it."

"Well, yeah, but I've been so busy and—"

"Spare us the excuses." Jess waved her off.

Excuses! Sienna opened her mouth, then snapped it shut. It wouldn't do to get into a snit with Jess right there in public.

She drew a deep breath, letting oxygen fill her lungs and flow into her bloodstream, as she'd learned to do

65

in a stress reduction workshop. For good measure she took another breath.

The breathing method helped, but the zingers from Jess and Cary still stung.

Was that what friends were for?

6

"Aw-woo! Aw-woo-woo-woo!" Liane Silverback and her husband, Wesley Loneheart, threw their heads back and howled.

Sienna watched, eyes wide. She had never seen adults—at least not human adults—howl in public before. Full-fledged, crooning, ear-ringing howls. This was probably a first, even for the Institute of the Inner Self.

Ending her howl with a little *woof woof* bark, Liane tossed her silver-gray hair over a shoulder. She had a large, freckled, pointy face, and every time she parted her lips Sienna noticed bright white teeth. "The song of the wolf is the song of freedom," she told the class, "and the song of joy. It is also the song of longing and of grief and of the great mysteries of life. It is the very soul of the wolf pouring forth."

Sienna's mother nodded. She sat cross-legged next to her daughter on the straw mat, wearing a beautiful crocheted vest. On the other side of Mom, Dad leaned back against the cushioned wall, thoughtfully rubbing his knees.

"The wolf," said Wesley, "expresses his or her feelings with complete honesty. There are no lies in the world of the wolf.''

''Join us now in the song of the wolf.'' Liane's blue eyes swept over the dozen workshop participants circled around her. ''You must open your hearts. No lies. The jaws open wide as a symbol of that complete openness. The teeth are bared before the howl to show the power and strength of the wolf heart.''

Sienna glanced at her parents, who were already dropping their jaws and baring their teeth. So was everyone else in the class. Except for her. She didn't feel a hundred percent sure about this. For one thing, she didn't see what howling had to do with Resolving Family Crisis, which was what the workshop was supposed to be about. After three arguments that week, her parents had finally realized that they had to do something. They enrolled in the workshop at the institute and asked Sienna to come, too.

''We want you to feel secure about what's happening,'' Mom had explained, ''to witness what we're doing to make our family stronger.''

''That's right,'' said Dad. ''When my parents bickered I felt alone and confused. We don't want to do that to you—leave you out in the cold.'' He pointed at the workshop brochure. ''It's supposed to bring the whole family into the healing process.''

Sienna thought that sounded great, but was pretty sure he had said *healing,* not howling.

Oh, well. It did look like fun. She threw her head back. After a minute of howling and yipping, she began to understand the importance of the wolf song. Her voice joined her mother's and father's and the others', rising and falling, sometimes blending in and sometimes standing out. It *did* feel like her soul pouring forth. It felt *wonderful!* She was singing, calling to the moon and the stars, proclaiming to the earth who she was!

Wesley made a circle with his arms to signal the end of the song.

"Oh, how liberating!" exclaimed Mom, shivering with excitement.

"Yes, such a rich experience!" cried another of the participants.

"Empowering," added a woman in a I BRAKE FOR UNICORNS T-shirt.

A man wearing a pyramid-shaped earring had tears in his eyes. "I've never experienced anything like it. I'm deeply moved."

"How about you, Jon?" Mom asked Dad.

"Yes, how did the wolf song make you feel?" asked Liane.

Dad leaned his head to the side, frowning. "It was . . . incomplete. I don't think I had finished my song yet."

"You mean when I motioned for the howling to end?" asked Wesley.

"Yes," Dad answered.

Liane rearranged the folds of her Mexican serape. "That brings up an important point. Each wolf sings a unique song, just as each of us does. In a family, when we're all singing different songs at once, trying to hear them all, putting them all together . . . sometimes it's difficult."

"Ah," said Dad, nodding, "yes." He glanced at Mom.

"Wolves make excellent families, though," said

69

Wesley. "They form lifelong bonds with pack mates. They take watchful care of their young. They share and play and work as a unit, for the good of the pack."

Liane nodded. "We have much to learn from the wolf. How deep are our commitments? How well do we care for our children?"

Sienna noticed her parents glance worriedly at each other, then at her. She gave them a reassuring smile. They took care of her just fine. It was *their* relationship she was worried about.

"Are we truly working together?" Wesley went on. "Or are we each working toward our own separate goals and ignoring those of our pack mates?"

Sienna gave that one some thought. Mom always complained that Dad was selfish in not doing more to promote his store. She said that when the store did poorly it put a strain on their finances, and if only he would come down off his high horse and do some advertising he'd get a lot more business. Did that count as ignoring the goals of the pack mates?

The instructors brought up some other qualities that humans could learn from wolves, then talked about one that made Sienna think really hard.

"Accepting criticism," said Liane, "is an important part of life in a wolf pack. There are scuffles and tussles among the wolves, but in a close-knit, smooth-functioning pack the fights are quick and honest and thorough. Wolves don't hold grudges. They fight fair and clear the air."

"It is usually the stronger wolf who fights the least often." Wesley stroked his graying beard. "When you know you are right, and you know that you are strong,

70

you have nothing to prove. It is beneath the dignity of a strong wolf to bicker over petty matters.''

Sienna nodded. How true. For instance, it would be beneath her dignity to bicker with Cary and Jess over the stingers they shot at her. Whenever she was a little late or had to miss a meeting or happened to forget about something ... Let them needle her all they wanted.

''Like the strong wolf, we can learn to accept criticism in stride and to forgive others in their uglier, meaner moments,'' counseled Liane.

Yes! Sienna agreed. She would forgive Jess and Cary in their uglier, meaner moments. She would be the strong wolf. What a fabulous breakthrough!

Fizzing with excitement, she turned to her parents. Mom was frowning at Dad and he was scowling back at her. Maybe they were trying to figure out who was the strong wolf.

They certainly hadn't seemed to reach any breakthroughs.

''*Phew!* Hi, everybody! Hi, Webb. Oops, I'm late. Hi, Sheela. What did I miss?'' Sienna hurried into Cary's garage Saturday morning, smiling, waving and humming the tune to ''Tomorrow'' to herself.

''You're *half an hour* late,'' Jess informed her as she passed.

''What you missed was half the meeting,'' Cary added.

Sienna shot smiles at each of them, adding another for Hallie, who was tapping her pencil on the table

71

impatiently. *Strong wolves don't fight,* she reminded herself.

"Why don't you get settled in, Sienna," said Hallie. "We've just started going over Save China Hill news. We'll fill you in on the rest later."

"Sure." She picked her way through the maze of Eco-kids, stepping over several Eco-juniors to get to her beanbag chair in the corner.

"Well, as I was saying"—Hallie sat forward—"It seems like Moreland and Mortimer just don't want to talk to us. I've left a million messages."

"Of course they don't," said Freedom. "They're stalling. They figure if they ignore us long enough, we'll go away."

"Well, we won't!" Sam Fong cried out. His Eco-junior pals joined in. "We won't! We won't!"

Sienna yawned. It came out much louder than she'd expected. Jess turned and glowered at her. She had to clamp a hand over her mouth to stifle another yawn. Her eyelids drooped and the rest of her body longed to curl up right there on the beanbag chair and go to sleep.

Getting to the meeting at all that morning had been a real accomplishment. Last night her parents had taken her with them to a new art gallery opening. They hadn't gotten home till midnight, and then she had trouble sleeping because of the excitement. Roger Phillips the baseball player had been there with Cindi Masterson the supermodel. He was ten times more handsome in person then on TV, and Cindi was much too skinny. Their autographs joined the others in Sienna's collection, which she had decided to get up and rearrange at 2 A.M. instead of tossing and turning.

Maybe if she just shut her eyes for a second or two she could catch a little nap during the meeting. Anyway, it was just a general meeting. All they ever did was rehash news from the different committees, most of which Sienna already knew because she was on two of them herself and always heard about the rest through the grapevine. And why did they have to hold these meetings so early in the day? Ten o'clock on a Saturday morning. Barbaric.

She shut her eyes. Just a little nap . . . one or two winks . . . a few *z*'s . . .

"Huh? What?" In what seemed like only a second later she woke to a jab in the ribs.

"Your head fell on my shoulder." Matt Parker, one of the Eco-juniors, scowled at her. "Wake up, will you?"

Sienna blinked, scowling back. Her head on Matt Parker's shoulder? Yuck! He was the kind of kid who always made cooties seem possible.

"Want me to wake you up if you nod off again?" asked Gina Chang, another Eco-junior. She smiled big, showing her missing front tooth.

"No, thanks. I'll be fine." Sienna shook her head. Pesky kids.

"The mayor's office finally called me back," Cary was saying. "Moreland and Mortimer does have the government permits to build on China Hill."

A groan rose from the group.

"But how can it be okay for them to build there?" wailed Sheela. "It's so beautiful. . . ."

"Apparently they convinced the government that it *is* okay," said Webb.

Derek scrunched up his face. "Companies like that have piles of money. They can do whatever they want."

"Why don't we call that marine mammal group that helped you rescue the dolphins last summer?" Kristin suggested. "Maybe they'd have some ideas on what to try next."

"That's a great idea!" agreed Hallie.

Cary nodded. "You know, you're right. Why should we Eco-kids have to fight this battle on our own? Other environmental groups would have to be interested, wouldn't they?"

Freedom waved a hand impatiently. "It's very simple. Go out there on China Hill. March around. Protest. Get on the TV news. Moreland and Mortimer will run away from the bad publicity and never be seen again."

"That's wishful thinking, Freedom," countered Webb. "I don't think this issue is as simple as the dolphin one was. Moreland and Mortimer probably have millions of dollars riding on this town house development. They're not going to give up without a real fight."

Sienna pulled her legs into a yoga position and did a few neck rotation exercises to stimulate her energy. Yes, that was better. She worked her shoulders next. It was during one of her shoulder extensions that she noticed two men walking up the driveway.

"Oh, Mr. Kingston! Hi!" called Cary.

"Hello." The older man nodded.

Sienna got up. "Hi, Mr. Kingston." She picked through the crowd to greet him. "Remember me? Sienna Sabo. Welcome to the Eco-kids."

He nodded. "Brought my neighbor Louis Gentry. He's the president of our homeowners association."

"The Diamond Court Homeowners Association." Mr. Gentry extended a hand to shake with the girls. He smiled, his white teeth a dazzle against his heavily tanned skin.

Sienna wondered whether he took tropical vacations, played a lot of tennis, or lived in a tanning salon. Maybe all three.

"I want you kids to know we're on your side." He smiled. "I understand you are opposed to building on China Hill. We're committed to helping you."

"All *right!*" chorused the Eco-kids.

Mr. Gentry beamed.

Tanning salon, Sienna decided. He was a trim guy of forty or so, blond, wearing an expensive blue suit.

"Well, shall we go over our strategy?" He walked up to the table, shoved aside Hallie's meeting notes and Jess's pocket datebook and popped open his leather briefcase. "Here's what I was thinking."

Sienna blinked, amazed. Out of the briefcase Mr. Gentry pulled a fistful of file folders, a gold pen, and a map.

"Hold this," he told Mr. Kingston.

Unfolded, the map was almost as big as Mr. Kingston. When he held it up all you could see of him were his straw hat at the top and his scruffy brown loafers at the bottom.

"Now. Here we have a bird's-eye view of the China Hill bluff." With his gold pen Mr. Gentry whacked at a spot in the middle of the map, somewhere around Mr. Kingston's belly button. "This is the area slated for development. Three quarter-acre parcels. And on each parcel they plan to build four town houses."

Webb nodded. 'We know. Moreland and Mortimer sent us a brochure—''

"And," Mr. Gentry cut in, "they plan to improve the path along the creek, to provide public access to the beach below, to install a public picnic area . . .''

"They also plan to build twelve town houses," Freedom reminded him sharply.

"China Hill won't be the same if they build on it," said Cary. "It's too tiny to be built on at all.''

Jess nodded. "That bluff is really important to our community. We go hiking there, whale watching, we have picnics. It's one of the few places around that's been left wild.''

"And it's pretty," added Sheela. "It's sad to think of it being ruined.''

Mr. Gentry flashed a smile. "You're a remarkable set of young people, aren't you?''

"How can we stop Moreland and Mortimer?" asked Vivian.

"Right," said Mr. Gentry, as if he had forgotten why he was there. "Why don't I show you?" He pulled another folder from his briefcase.

Sienna crossed her arms. She didn't feel good about this, and wasn't sure why. There was just something about this man.

He took out a sheet of paper. "Here's my idea. They probably expect for you to do things like, you know, get a petition going, write letters to the government demanding to protect the bluff . . . that sort of thing. But I say, take them by surprise. Do something different, and do it *now*.''

"Yeah!" Nate agreed.

76

Freedom was nodding enthusiastically.

Sienna frowned. They didn't even know what they were agreeing to.

"Do *what* exactly?" she asked. Somebody had to be levelheaded about this.

"Why, public relations, of course," Mr. Gentry replied. "We hold a press conference. We get television, radio, newspapers out there at the bluff. Show them what we mean."

Press conference. The words fluttered about Sienna's mind like colorful birds. Television . . . radio . . . newspapers . . . Wonderful, magic words. Sienna Sabo, the Eco-kids' starring spokeswoman, representing their cause to millions of viewers . . .

Maybe this wasn't such a bad idea, after all.

7

It was probably the coldest day of the year. The sky hovered low and slate gray. Wind whipped at the sea, churning the waves into white foam. Then it gusted up China Hill through the bluff's dry winter brush and grasses.

It also turned Sienna's hair into a fright wig. She tried holding onto it with one hand while clutching her speech notes in the other.

The weather hadn't stopped forty-seven people from showing up for the Eco-kids' Save China Hill press conference. Sienna knew how many there were because Jess had counted them—and reported a new count whenever more arrived.

"What a turnout!" Cary eyes were wide.

Web nodded. "Our flyers must have worked."

"The Eco-juniors passed them out through the whole neighborhood," little Gina declared proudly.

"Look, the reporters!" Derek pointed at the street. "There's the Channel Six news van."

"I called every reporter who's ever covered the Eco-kids," Sienna explained. "Freddy Fredemeyer at Channel Six, Abe Taylor at the *Jewel Beach Journal*, Deborah

78

Roth from KUJB radio . . . They were all very interested in this.'' She grinned smugly. What a thrill it was to dial the reporters' numbers, tell them what the club was up to, and have them pounce eagerly on the story. She loved it.

''What time is it, Jess?'' she asked.

Jess pushed some buttons on her electronic watch. ''I'm setting the alarm. It's nine forty-two. Eighteen minutes till we're supposed to start.''

In other words, eighteen minutes until Sienna had to go onstage. She would stand next to the Warning. No Trespassing! sign there at the top of the bluff on Diamond Court, introduce her club, and talk about why they wanted to save China Hill. All this in front of forty-seven people plus the TV, radio, and newspaper audiences.

She pushed her shoulders back to open her rib cage and lungs, to fill them with oxygen.

''Hey, where's Mr. Gentry?'' asked Vivian.

Webb searched the crowd. ''I haven't see him yet.''

''But there's Mr. Kingston,'' Ramon pointed out.

He was talking with an elderly couple under a pine tree. All three of them held onto their hats against the wind.

''Seems like Mr. Gentry at least got lots of the Diamond Court Homeowners Association members to come out,'' noted Nate. ''Look at all these people.''

''Well, half of them are Eco-kids and Eco-juniors,'' Cary pointed out.

Jess shook her head. ''Not quite. There are twenty-one of us today, which is closer to one-third of the total.''

"Leave it to Jess to do the statistics." Ramon rolled his eyes.

"It's okay," Sienna defended her. "We're going to need an accurate head count to give the news people. They love to put things like that in their stories."

"Like this . . ." Ramon pretended to hold a microphone. He made his voice deep. "Forty-seven citizens turned out for an Eco-kids press conference today at China Hill in Jewel Beach. It was a blustery winter day, but that didn't stop them from staying to listen to—"

"Oh, here comes Freddy!" Sienna interrupted him. She waved to a short man wearing an orange bow tie.

The reporter hurried toward them, trailing his camera crew. But midway there he was blocked by a blond woman in a business suit. Two men in business suits flanked her while she spoke to Freddy. He started writing things down in his reporter's notebook.

"Wonder who *they* are." Vivian frowned.

"I'll go see." Sienna had taken only one step when Jess grabbed her arm.

"Oh, no you don't." Cary shook her head, smiling. "You'll get stuck over there talking and we'll never get the press conference started."

Sienna pursed her lips. "Nice to know you two have such faith in me."

"Of course we do," Jess assured her. "You're the best spokesperson around. We're not about to lose track of you."

"Then one of *us* would have to make the speech," said Hallie, pretending to bite her nails.

"Hah! That would be a laugh!" Sam slapped his knee.

80

"Eight minutes to go," Jess warned with a glance at her watch.

"Where *is* Louis Gentry?" Vivian wondered aloud. "He said he'd be here."

Sienna shrugged. "We don't really need him." She wrinkled her nose. "I'm not sure I like the way he takes over, anyway."

"You mean you don't think this press conference was a good idea?" Cary asked her. "I think it's great. Look how many people have shown up."

"No, it is great, but . . ." Sienna wasn't sure where to begin. She had no specific evidence against Mr. Gentry and couldn't really explain why she doubted him. Just a funny feeling. In a Language Through Silence seminar they had said you should pay attention to funny feelings. Intuition, sixth sense, whatever you wanted to call it . . . Sometimes it was your own personal alarm system going off.

"I know, you just want to have the speech all to yourself, Sienna." Ramon grinned. "You don't want to share the spotlight. That's why you don't mind Gentry not being here, right? This way he won't horn in on your moment of glory, huh?"

Sienna played along. "However did you guess, Ramon? You are just so clever."

"Well, five minutes and counting," Jess informed them. "Why don't we go ahead and take our places?"

Hallie waved her arm to signal the group, and Ramon herded up some straggling Eco-juniors. They all moved together toward the Keep Out! sign.

Sienna made her way to the front of the group. At times like these it helped to be tall, because not only

81

could she see but everyone could see her, too. To be sure of it, she had worn her brightest colors—a tangerine jumper and turtleneck over lime green lights. Her hair always helped, too. The wind picked it up like a long auburn banner.

She knew she stood out in a crowd. That was exactly how she wanted it.

"Good morning, everyone!" she shouted above the wind. "Thanks for coming!"

In a moment the crowd quieted and gathered closer.

"My name is Sienna Sabo and our club is the Eco-kids." She noticed the Channel Six camera swing on her. Both Freddy Fredemeyer and the radio reporter rushed up to hold the microphones in her face. Immediately, her jitters calmed. Her delight in being center stage took over. "We're having this press conference today because we're very worried about this place right here, China Hill." She waved at the land behind her.

Cary stood on her left, nodding. Jess was there, too, and on her right side stood Ramon and Freedom. A backup of friends always helped.

"People other than us are also worried about it," she said, "like the Diamond Court Homeowners Association, who live right next to China Hill on this street. How many of you are here?"

Mr. Kingston and his two elderly friends raised their hands.

Sienna smiled. "Anyone else?"

The crowd of strangers stared silently back at her.

"Oh." She glanced at Cary and Jess, puzzled. "Well, anyway, a company called Moreland and Mortimer

82

wants to build town houses up here and we don't think that's a good idea. China Hill is a—''

"Why the heck not?" someone shouted.

"Pardon me?" Sienna peered through the crowd.

A man in a red ski jacket stepped forward. "I said, what's wrong with building new homes? This town needs new homes. And I need a job building them." His face bore an angry flush as red as his jacket.

"Well, maybe," Sienna continued, "but I was just about to say that China Hill is a very beautiful place, as you can see, and it needs to be preserved."

The woman beside the man put her hands on her hips. "How about people who want homes? What about people who want to buy up here."

Sienna gulped. What was going on? Who were these people? Not reporters, as far as she could tell.

"Ignore them," Freedom counseled in a whisper. "Go on with your speech."

Sienna glanced at the next notecard in the stack that the Save China Hill committee had written up for her. "In our community China Hill has been an important place for recreation and appreciation of nature for many years. There aren't many wild areas left in Jewel Beach and we shouldn't destroy one more."

"Is that all you care about? Wild areas?" asked an old man. "What about people? People need jobs. People need homes."

"Exactly. I need a home," added a woman in a gray trench coat. "I grew up in Jewel Beach and I've been trying to move back here for years, but haven't been able to find the right house."

83

"Just keep talking," Ramon whispered in Sienna's ear. "Don't let them take over."

He was right. This was turning into a free-for-all.

"Excuse me." Sienna smiled. "If you'll let me finish what I have to say, then we can—"

The man in the ski jacket broke in again. "You kids better just give up. We're not going to let you stop this construction."

"What business is it of yours, anyway?" demanded the old man. "You're just a bunch of nosy do-gooders."

Sienna's eyes went wide. The heat of anger raced up her spine. "Nosy do-gooders?" she repeated. Who *were* these people? Where were all the Diamond Court homeowners who were supposed to show up and support the Eco-kids?

Jess leaned toward her and whispered, "Don't let them get your goat, okay? Stay calm."

Sienna took in a deep breath. "Let's not interrupt each other," she began again. "What the Eco-kids are trying to say is that China Hill isn't just any piece of land. It's very special."

"*Eco*-kids!" huffed a young woman. "What do you kids know about ecology? All you're doing is jumping on the ecology bandwagon. You just want attention. To get popular. It's the thing to do these days, isn't it?"

"These town houses are going to provide jobs for the people who build them and homes for the people who buy them," said the woman in the trench coat.

"Yeah, who are *you,* anyway, little girl?" the older man pointed right at Sienna. "Some spoiled rich kid who has nothing better to do than meddle in other people's business." He laughed and elbowed the man next to him.

Rich kid? Sienna was flabbergasted. *Nothing better to do?* Before she could form a reply, Ramon came up with one first.

"Hey, mister," he called out, "you're way out of line. Why don't you hear what our spokesperson has to say before you call us names?"

"Yeah," Freedom joined in. "Be quiet and let her talk!"

The strong wolf knows she's right and doesn't have to fight, Sienna reminded herself. There had to be a way to calm these people down, to get them to listen. She waited several seconds before saying anything, letting her eyes roam over the crowd. Why were they so angry?

Her gaze met Freddy Fredemeyer's. He looked worried about her, as if he wanted to speak up and help her himself.

But it was old Mr. Kingston who suddenly appeared beside the Eco-kids.

"Now, look here," he shouted. "These youngsters have something to say and you'd better mind your manners and let them say it." He held his hat out like a shield. His bushy gray eyebrows met over his snub of a nose. Determination had changed him from quiet old man to snarling bulldog.

He was absolutely the last person Sienna would have expected to come to the rescue.

8

"This is infuriating," said Sienna's mother.

"Shh!" Dad frowned. "I want to hear it."

"These children," said the blond woman in a business suit, "though sincere, are misguided." She smiled into Freddy Fredemeyer's camera, and the smile flowed into the Sabo-Engstrom family's living room through the TV.

Sienna felt sick. All the joy she had experienced in anticipation of being on the six o'clock news had fizzled. Worse than fizzled. Fried.

"As president of of Moreland and Mortimer Development Corporation, I, Nora Robb, want to make it clear that our company is very concerned about environmental issues. The China Hill town homes will be built with the utmost respect for the natural setting."

"Plus, we'll provide a picnic area and a nature trail for public access to the beach below," added the man next to her. "I'm Kendall Kirstner, principal architect, and I'll personally oversee the construction process."

Freddy Fredemeyer pulled the microphone back to himself. "But the Eco-kids feel that China Hill should remain the way it is now. And they charge that you've refused to discuss your plans with them."

"We're well known in the home-building industry for our integrity and responsibility." Nora smiled. "We'll do nothing to harm the local community. If anything, we aim to enhance it by providing employment and new homes."

The videotape cut to Sienna's speech. There were close-ups of her and of the angry faces of the crowd. The man in the ski jacket, the older man, and the woman in the trench coat shouted Sienna down again and again.

"Oh, how rude!" Mom hissed.

Sienna sank deep into the sofa, shutting her eyes.

Mom's arm slipped around her. On the other side, Dad took her hand.

"It's all right, darling," Mom whispered.

"They're making *themselves* look bad," added Dad.

Still, Sienna wished she could somehow make the news program disappear. Or the *whole day* disappear.

Mr. Kingston stood up and defended her, and then at last Sienna was able to finish her speech. But by then the whole tone of the press conference had changed. Now the Eco-kids were on the defense. Instead of forcing Moreland and Mortimer to respond to their questions, *they* were the ones who had been on the spot.

Finally Freddy Fredemeyer spoke up. "Maybe the Eco-kids would like to ask the representatives from Moreland and Mortimer some questions." But the camera found the blond woman and the two men climbing into a limousine. They glided away.

The news tape cut to Freddy standing at the top of the bluff beside the Keep Out! sign, with sweeping views of the meadow and the wind-tossed sea in the background. "Construction is scheduled to begin in two months," he said, "unless public outcry causes government agencies to reconsider Moreland and Mortimer's permit to build here. Up to this point it hasn't seemed likely to happen, but maybe with this new public interest things will change."

Sienna blinked. "Huh?"

Freddy Fredemeyer went on. "I was unable to speak on the record with any officials, but an informed source has told me that the city and county are taking another look at the permits granted to Moreland and Mortimer."

Sienna sat up straight. "Wow!"

Dad squeezed her hand.

"It is interesting to note," said Freddy, "that this is the third time in less than a year that this group of young people has been involved in important environmental projects. They have taken on challenges that adults have been unable or unwilling to face. Last August they convinced officials at Aquarius Marine Park to turn two wild dolphins being held there over to a marine mammal rescue group. Those dolphins, known as Leon and Tamara, now live in an ocean preserve where they are being prepared to live in the wild again."

The tape switched from him to old clips of the Eco-kids at work on neighborhood recycling day.

"The Eco-kids have also started successful recycling programs in their school and neighborhood," Freddy's voice narrated. "In fact, when news reports about those recycling programs appeared on this station, city officials were embarrassed to realize that children were doing things that *they* should do. City council has voted to start a city-wide recycling program next year." Freddy's grinning face came back on the screen.

"Whether the Eco-kids are right or wrong about saving China Hill, we've all got to hand it to them for spunk."

The camera panned to a shot of some of the Eco-kids gathered at the top of the bluff under a stormy sky, prevented by the Keep Out! sign from entering China Hill.

"This is Freddy Fredemeyer for Channel Six News."

Sienna gasped. "Wow!"

"Wow, indeed." Dad smiled.

Mom hugged her. "You did a wonderful job, darling. Grace under pressure, to say the least."

"Just like a professional," said Dad. "Congratulations. You made them look like raving idiots, just by standing your ground."

"Really?" Sienna smiled.

"I'm still very angry about how you were treated, though." Mom crossed her arms.

"Those hecklers ... It makes me want to break heads," Dad fumed. "I'm sorry I wasn't there, sweetheart."

Mom shook her head. "If I'd had any idea it would be that way ..."

"Thanks." Sienna hugged them both. "It was awful. I'm so embarrassed. They kept interrupting me and I didn't know what to say. I mean, I'm not even on the Save China Hill committee. I was just the spokesperson they chose to make the little speech. And we were all taken by surprise. We had no idea those people would be there or the people from Moreland and Mortimer."

"Why *were* they there?" asked Mom. "How did they find out about your press conference?"

"Freddy told them," Sienna answered. "He apologized afterward for not letting us know. He said he called them for comment before the press conference. It's standard practice. But he was sorry he hadn't warned us.''

''And I guess Moreland and Mortimer got those people to show up.'' Dad rubbed his knees, thinking. ''Those extremely unpleasant individuals who heckled you.''

Sienna nodded. ''Exactly. They planned the whole thing.''

''How about that fellow who planned the press conference for you? The Diamond Court Homeowners Association president, did you say?'' Mom asked her. ''How did he feel about how things turned out?''

''He wasn't there.'' Sienna shrugged. ''He never showed up.''

''You're kidding!'' Dad frowned. ''He sets it all up, then sends you kids out there to take the lumps alone?''

Sienna reached over to scoop Number One off the ottoman. ''Actually, I've been wondering the same thing. He was so gung-ho about the press conference, then didn't even bother to show up. And only three people from the homeowners association were there.''

''How very odd,'' said Mom.

Rubbing Number One's tummy, Sienna nodded. ''I know. I think I need to find out more about this, don't I? I'm going to talk to Jess and Cary.''

During the next hour she tried dialing Cary's number three times and then Jess's. Both lines stayed busy. Then it was time for dinner. Dad cooked her favorite dish, basil fettuccine with homemade Alfredo sauce, and her mother didn't even say anything when she fed a few strands of it to Number One under the table. After the pasta, plus the banana ice cream sundaes Mom put together for them, Sienna felt relaxed and peaceful for the first time all day. The last thing she felt like doing was calling Cary and Jess to rehash the press conference and get all tense again.

It could wait till tomorrow.

But when tomorrow came, Dad wanted to drive to a Buddhist retreat in the desert so they could ''center'' themselves spiritually, because it had been such a challenging week. The three of them spent the day sitting in hot mineral water pools and gazing at cactus and distant mountains.

On Monday morning she overslept and had to tell Cary and Jess to walk to school without her. At lunch Mandy and Tara wanted her to sit with them to plan a surprise birthday party for Kendra. After lunch there was a drama club meeting to discuss the district competition in May. A dress rehearsal for the recycling skits ran from after school till dinner time. Then, during dinner her whole world split open like a watermelon and broke in two.

''You didn't add salt to this soup, did you, Liv?'' Dad asked.

Mom shook her head. ''The herbs give it plenty of flavor.''

''It's bland,'' said Dad. ''I always salt a vegetable-based soup.''

''Good for you,'' answered Mom.

''What's that supposed to mean?''

''Just what I said, Jon. If you want it salty, go ahead and salt it.''

Dad looked at her. "It's best if it's done during the simmering."

Mom took an angry bite out of her roll.

"What is it, Liv?" Dad demanded. "I've had it with your surliness tonight."

"Surly? *Me* surly? You're the one who ..."

"Who what?" Dad's blue eyes flashed. "What did I do this time?"

"You know exactly what you did."

Dad worked his jaw. "You're angry that I told Chris Madsen that I don't want advertising space in his new home decorating magazine."

"Angry, I'm afraid, is not the right word. Chris is our friend, and he offered you the first two months at half price. I think I'm beyond anger now." Mom looked at him.

"What do you mean?" Dad asked.

"Maybe we shouldn't have this discussion here." Mom covered Sienna's hand with her own. "There's something we've been considering, and ... Should Dad and I go to another room?"

"I would prefer that we talk about this openly," Dad countered, "so that Sienna won't experience fear of the unknown. But, Sienna, if you'd prefer, we could ..."

She shook her head. "No. What have you been considering?"

Mom sighed. "Well, your father and I have been running into disagreements we can't resolve, and it's making us very angry with each other, so ..."

"We talked about ... about living apart for a little while," said Dad, "so that we can each have some space to think things through in a calm environment."

92

Mom nodded. "Without bumping into each other all the time and intensifying our problems. A little time apart."

"Time apart?" Sienna repeated hoarsely.

She tried her best to understand. She tried to accept what her parents were saying, and have faith in their ability to make the right decision. But she couldn't. Her eyes got cloudy and within seconds they were puddles of tears. "Don't you *love* each other?"

"Oh, darling, of course we do." Mom got up and came around the table to hug her.

"Very much so," Dad added, patting her shoulder. "Very much. That's why we're eager to do whatever must be done to work things out."

"Then—" Sienna sniffled. "Then you've decided? You're going to . . . to have this time apart thing?"

Through blurry eyes she saw her parents look at each other.

"Actually . . ." Dad shook his head. "No. We haven't decided. Sometimes *I* feel we should go through with it, and sometimes your mother does, but we never seem to feel it at the same time."

Mom smiled. "It's a little funny, I suppose. We can't even seem to agree on *this*."

Sienna's tears subsided long enough for a shade of a grin to sneak though. Here was one question where she was glad her parents didn't see eye to eye.

At seven o'clock the next morning Sienna's radio alarm went off, blasting the voice of Sinbad, the Master of the Morning, as the deejay called himself, into her room. She reached over, fumbled around for the snooze button, and punched it. Ten minutes later a U2 song came on. Eventually, long after U2 had finished and some oldies tune was playing, Sienna opened one eye. The large green numbers on the clock said 7:25. Bad news. She *had* to get up now.

Curled up beside her on the comforter, Number One lifted his eyelids just enough to take a look at her. Then he yawned, stretched, and fell asleep again.

"I'm jealous," she told him, scratching behind his ear. "How about you go to school and I'll stay home and catnap?"

When she finally swung her legs over the side of the bed, her head felt stuffed with rags. Well, no wonder, with all the emotional turmoil last night—crying at the dinner table, and later she was too worried to fall asleep. Even after she did fall asleep a horrible nightmare woke her. Sienna couldn't quite remember what it was, but it must have symbolized her anxiety over her parents' relationship.

The very thought of "time apart" made her want to cry again. Would they go through with it? If they did, where would they each go? Who would she live with?

The doorbell rang at seven thirty-five. Mom and Dad had both left early, so Sienna had to answer it herself. Through the peephole she saw two familiar faces.

"You're early!" she told Cary and Jess, pulling the door open for them.

Cary shrugged. "Just five minutes."

"Five minutes is five minutes." Sienna motioned them to her room. "I'm not ready yet."

"So what else is new?" grumbled Jess.

Sienna ignored her. "Just let me pull some clothes on."

In Sienna's room, Cary beelined for Number One and picked him up for a hug. "He's so beautiful," she cooed. "Like a show kitty, aren't you? It's hard to believe that he and my Tolkien are brothers. Tolk is more the alley cat type—stripy, skinny, and sneaky."

Jess nodded. "Amazing that my cat is this one's sister. Curie hardly ever sleeps. She's our home inspector. Explores and investigates everything."

"Sleeping is Number One's favorite hobby. Isn't it, love?" Cary held him upside down in her arms, baby-style, while Jess rubbed under his chin.

They fawned over him for a couple more minutes before Jess made a point of looking at her watch. "Almost ready, Sienna?"

"What do you think of this?" Sienna modeled her outfit. Red wool sweater, red plaid leggings, her hair held back by a big red bow.

"Nice," said Jess.

Cary smiled. "Pretty."

Turning back to the mirror, Sienna shook her head. "This color is wrong on me today. I'm already too red. My eyes are all puffy and—"

"Sienna, you look fine," Jess interrupted, "and I don't want to be late to school. Can we just go?"

"Don't you even care about what I was going to say? Why my eyes look puffy?" Sienna stared at her. This wasn't a good idea—picking a fight with Jess—but she couldn't help herself. She needed a shoulder to cry on about last night's scary news and her friends were being no help at all.

95

"At the moment," Jess replied stonily, "I care a lot more about getting to school on time."

"How about if we talk on the way to school?" Cary suggested.

It had been ages since Cary had jumped in to settle one of their disputes. Sienna gave it some thought. Did she want to keep up the old bickering forever?

Jess must have been asking herself the same question. "I didn't mean to snap at you," she said. "I do care about what you had to say. But can you just wear what you're wearing and hurry up?"

Sienna sighed. "Oh, all right. I'm ready."

On the way out she grabbed her books off her desk and slipped on a pair of loafers. She'd rather have worn her red ankle boots, but they'd take too long to lace up. Actually, she'd rather have worn blue today. Blue, like her mood. But for the sake of harmony in her friendships, red would have to do.

"Now," said Cary as they started down the sidewalk, "what were you going to tell us?"

"Oh." Sienna sighed. "It's something I'm feeling very sad about."

"The press conference," Jess guessed. "You're not the only one. What a disaster."

"You haven't been around much," Cary added, "so we haven't been able to talk with you about it, but—"

Sienna shook her head. "I tried calling both of you that night and your lines were busy."

Cary shrugged. "Maybe it was when we were trying to call you."

"We thought you were talking to your drama club

friends or something," said Jess. "You seem to spend a lot of time with them." Her tone was a little sharp.

Sienna raised an eyebrow. "Is that a problem?"

"I know you have other friends. That's not a problem," said Jess.

Sienna felt relieved. "Well, what *is* the problem, then?"

Cary bunched her lips together, thinking. "It's like . . . like you don't really care too much about the Eco-kids. I mean, I know I'm probably *too* involved in it, and I don't expect everyone else to be. But couldn't you just show up for the things you say you're going to?"

"Like what?" Sienna frowned. "I show up."

Jess shook her head. "Not always."

"Like Monday," said Cary.

"What was Monday?" Sienna felt like a suspect under investigation. Jess and Cary were the police detectives on the case. On *her* case.

Cary put her hands in her jeans pockets. "See, you forgot all about it, didn't you? We asked you to come to an emergency Eco-kids meeting yesterday afternoon. We agreed to hold one to talk about the bombed press conference, remember?"

Sienna blushed. "Oh. I did forget. It's been a really busy couple of days. Worse than busy, actually. I—" She was about to tell them about her parents' possible split, but Jess broke in again.

"Sienna," she said, frowning, "if you want out of the Eco-kids, you should just say so." Jess looked her right in the eye.

Cary stared at her, too, making her feel like a bug under

a microscope. Jess and Cary, the ever-inquisitive scientists.

A small fireball of anger rolled around in Sienna's belly. It had been sparking all weekend. The pressure from the press conference, from her parents' problems, and now being picked on by the very friends she had turned to for comfort. It was all adding up to something explosive.

There were a million things she wanted to shriek at Cary and Jess—angry and hurt and confused things. But what came out of her mouth in the iciest possible voice was something she didn't even mean.

"Yes, Jess. You're right. Maybe I should."

Naturally, the next afternoon Sienna had hot-line duty. Life always worked that way. Very inconvenient. If her shift had been scheduled for later in the week instead, she could have had a few more days to let Cary and Jess stew. This way, she'd *have* to see them.

In the meantime, she avoided them. During lunch she sat with her drama club friends. Whenever she spotted Jess or Cary in the halls she looked the other way.

It was very tempting to skip hot-line duty. Call in sick or something. Which was probably just what Cary and Jess expected her to do. They always seemed to expect the worst from her, anyway.

Well, she wouldn't give them that satisfaction.

She made it to Cary's only two minutes late. The Save China Hill committee was there for their regular meeting, but with much smaller attendance than usual. Only a half dozen Eco-kids sat at the table.

To Sienna's surprise, everyone smiled and said hello when she came in—including Jess and Cary.

"Hi, everybody," she replied, forcing a cheerful note into her voice.

No sooner had she settled in at the hot-line desk than a call came in from a woman with a shy parrot.

"He won't say anything but 'Oh! Pardon me' in just a whisper," the caller complained.

"Do *you* say that a lot?" Sienna asked out of curiosity.

"Well, I don't know. Maybe I—Oh, pardon me, will you? Someone's at the door."

Sienna waited till the woman came back, then gave her the phone number for a bird behaviorist she found listed in the hot-line notebook. After that came a couple of calls with routine puppy care questions. She wrote their addresses on envelopes and promised to mail them information packets.

The hot line stayed busy after that, one call after another. When a breather came she had to seal all the envelopes, lick the stamps, and stack them in the out basket for the Eco-juniors to mail. Money they made from the recycling programs paid for the postage.

Sienna sighed. Why had she made that stupid remark about quitting the Eco-kids? That wasn't at all what she wanted to do. She loved the club. Why did things like that pop out of her mouth? Maybe if Cary and Jess hadn't been so hard on her, questioning her like a criminal . . .

Out of the corner of her eye she caught a glimpse of her friends. Cary's glum face rested in her palms, her elbows propped so low that her chin almost touched the table. Not the picture of joy. At the other end of the table, Jess leaned back in an old metal chair donated by Ramon's mom. Two deep lines of worry scored her forehead.

"I think we should try to understand why this happened," Webb was saying. "We won't get anywhere if we don't know what went wrong."

"We're not going to get anywhere anyway." Nate shook his head. "Let's just throw in the towel and go after a problem we know we can solve."

"My father says we fell for eco-chic," Jess reported.

"Which is what?" asked Webb.

"Oh, you know, 'chic' as in fashionable. He says maybe we got so enthusiastic about China Hill because we thought it was going to be a popular cause that other people would join in and help us on. Then we'd get pats on the back and everyone would think we were great."

"I wasn't thinking about pats on the back." Cary frowned. "I was thinking about China Hill. I want it to stay the way it is."

"Same here," echoed Freedom. "It's got to."

"Well, maybe we did go for the press conference too soon." Hallie shrugged. "I mean, we didn't think it through very well. It sounded great, and, I don't know . . . kind of glamorous or something. Being on TV."

Sienna thought about that. The idea of being on TV sure had drawn *her* into saving China Hill. Before Louis Gentry had shown up with his plan, she hadn't been so interested. She had even wondered if they *should* save China Hill.

Which reminded her . . . What about Louis Gentry? Where was he during that press conference?

"Well, anyway," said Nate, "I think we ought to cut our losses. Give up on China Hill. We're spending a lot of time on it, and it looks like the cards are stacked against us. It's burning people out, too. Look how few

101

Save China Hill committee members showed up for this meeting and for the emergency Eco-kids meeting on Monday.''

Give up? Sienna repeated to herself. Why give up? She hadn't planned to speak during this meeting, still feeling miffed at Cary and Jess. But her mouth wouldn't stay shut. ''I don't understand,'' she said.

Everyone turned to look at her.

''Why are you guys so grim about China Hill? Freddy Fredemeyer said on TV that our press conference might make the government people reconsider the building permit.''

Freedom waved a hand. ''That's old news. Freddy called Cary the other day and said that they're not going to take back the permit after all.''

Cary nodded. ''He explained that no politician or anyone like that wants to fight Moreland and Mortimer right now. The economy is bad and people don't have enough jobs. This would give jobs to construction workers. And those people who yelled at us during the press conference? Freddy says they were for real. They really do want construction jobs and homes up there and they're willing to fight for them.''

''So are we just going to roll over and play dead?'' asked Sienna.

All faces turned toward her.

''Sometimes when things look the worst is when you have the best chance for progress,'' she told them.

''Says who?'' asked Nate.

''Well, actually, it was in a seminar called Maximizing Your Ambition. See, when you come to a brick wall it forces you to get creative and think about your goal

102

in a different way. Where are you really trying to go? What are you really trying to achieve?''

''This is a pretty tall brick wall,'' Webb pointed out. ''I'm not saying we should quit, but Mortimer and Moreland is a very powerful company around here. They've got connections, as my mother says.''

''Connections to who?'' asked Cary.

Webb shrugged. ''The usual. Rich people, important people, people who make the decisions.''

''Well, maybe we have connections, too,'' proposed Sienna, ''and we just haven't connected with them yet. Like your mom and dad, for instance, Webb. They're rich and important, right?''

Webb blushed, then laughed. ''They're real estate agents. Their connections, unfortunately, are not with people who would be on our side. They're helpful for getting information about all this, but they're not real nuts about our stopping that construction on China Hill.''

''There must be something . . .'' Sienna gazed out the garage door into a sky just starting to turn pink with the sunset. Looking at the sky always helped her think.

''Our connection with the Diamond Court Homeowners Association did us a fat lot of good,'' Hallie pointed out. ''Three homeowners showed up.''

''I still haven't been able to reach Louis Gentry,'' Jess reported. ''I've left a half dozen messages on his machine.''

Sienna frowned. ''Don't you think that's a little weird?''

''Maybe he's on a business trip,'' Nate suggested.

''He's on *some* kind of trip,'' said Sienna.

Jess turned toward her. "What do you mean?"

"I sensed something fishy about him from the beginning. I mean, in this other seminar I took called Language Through Silence they talked about not letting your brain get in the way of your gut." Any minute now, Sienna knew, Jess was going to make fun of her. Jess hated her theories. But she went on anyway. "When you have a gut feeling about somebody, you should pay attention."

To Sienna's surprise, Jess nodded. "Actually, it's quite logical. Usually there's something very concrete that gives you your impression. For instance, a shifty look in someone's eye or whatever. You might not register the evidence at first, but on some level it stays with you."

Sienna's eyes widened. Jess was agreeing with her on this? Amazing! As soon as she got home she'd check her astrology chart. Maybe her stars and Jess's were reaching harmonic orbits.

"He did seem awful slick." Hallie frowned. "I mean, he talked us right into that press conference. . . ."

Webb nodded. "There must be a way to find out what's going on with Gentry. I'll ask my parents what they know about him and the homeowners association."

"I could talk to Mr. Kingston," offered Cary. "Maybe he knows why Gentry didn't show up."

A tingle ran up Sienna's spine. She loved the feeling of working together with her friends, of cooperating and sharing talents. Maybe her biggest contribution had been getting the committee fired up again. It was something like running her own Maximizing Your Ambition seminar.

It made her feel so good that she wanted to march right over to Cary and Jess and apologize for their misunderstanding the day before. But the hot-line phone rang again, and then the meeting ended, and after everybody else left, Cary and Jess got to her first.

"I'm really glad you were here," Cary told her. "You kept us from giving up."

Jess nodded. "You made some good suggestions."

"I don't want to quit the Eco-kids," Sienna confessed. "I never did."

"I figured." Cary smiled.

"I'm glad you don't want to quit." Jess nodded. "Your being late and whatnot annoys me, but you do work hard when you're here."

"So you don't *want* me to quit?"

"No!" said Jess. "I just hate waiting for you. It gets to me."

Sienna grinned. "Strangely enough, I've noticed. Don't know how I figured it out. Must just be intuition." She laughed. "But I want to say ... I'm sorry I'm always late and stuff. I'm trying to learn to accept constructive criticism." She was beginning to realize that you couldn't always be a strong wolf. Sometimes you had to really listen to what your friends said to you. "Maybe ... maybe there's a seminar or something I can take to work on that. Combating Your Tardiness or something."

Cary made her eyes wide. "Uh-oh. The seminar would never be the same again. Sienna Sabo attacks the lateness seminar!"

"Teacher encounters the ultimate challenge!" Jess joined in. "Admits defeat! Jumps off nearest bridge!"

Sienna crossed her arms. "All right, funny, funny. The queens of comedy."

"Well, okay," said Cary. "I'll talk about *my* problem now. I know I'm still too gung-ho about the club. I need to calm down. I just want to accomplish everything right away, you know? Save the earth *today*. And I think everybody else should want to, too."

"Why not?" Sienna raised her fist. "Let's do it! Save the world!"

"Easier said than done, is the problem. You get burned out when it doesn't happen," said Jess.

"Yeah, like half the committee today," Cary pointed out. "They didn't even show."

Sienna plopped down in the beanbag chair. "Bummer. But we're plunging on, right? China Hill hasn't been built on yet!"

Jess nodded and sank into a chair. "Not *yet*."

"Know what I think?" Cary perched on the edge of the table. "I think there shouldn't be an Eco-kids."

"Huh?" Sienna and Jess wondered in unison.

"We shouldn't have to exist." Cary crossed her arms. "I mean, why should kids have to do this stuff? Convince adults to recycle, to be kind to animals, to leave beautiful wild places wild . . ."

Sienna shrugged. "Somebody's got to do it."

"But why don't *they*? Adults are the ones who made this mess, not us."

Jess nodded. "My grandmother said something similar when I first told her about the Eco-kids club. She said it was her generation and others that mucked things up, then they left it up to ours to clean up after them."

"Well, I'm sick of it." Cary sighed. "We shouldn't

106

have to do all this work. Plus, they're always trying to stop us. And they might even win on China Hill.''

''Boy, sounds like you really are burned out,'' said Sienna.

Cary sighed again. ''I guess so.''

''Well, I haven't been working as hard on it as you have. I've been distracted by the drama club and . . . other stuff . . .'' She realized she hadn't told them about her parents' problem yet. But this didn't seem like the right time. ''So, anyway, I could be your motivational counselor.''

''My what?''

''She wants to play psychiatrist,'' Jess translated.

Sienna rolled her eyes. ''Wrong. More like . . . cheerleader.''

''She wants to be an Eco-kids cheerleader,'' Jess tried again.

''Yeah.'' Sienna nodded. ''I'll keep you up when the chips are down. I mean, I don't know about the other Eco-kids, but I know I can cheer up *you* two.''

Cary smiled. ''I guess you already have.''

Jess smiled, too. ''I may not often agree with you, Sienna, but you do come up with interesting ideas. To say the least.''

''Good.'' Sienna nodded. ''It's my goal in life to make things interesting. Boredom should be outlawed.''

''In that case . . . I should let you know about something.'' Cary's grin grew mischievous.

''What?'' Sienna eyed her suspiciously.

''Well . . . um . . .''

''*What,* Cary?''

''Well . . . you know how you always stare at Buck?''

107

Sienna blinked. "Whatever do you mean?"

"Oh, come on," Jess urged. "You know. The puppy dog eyes."

"Okay, okay. So what?" Sienna's heartbeat picked up. Actually, she hadn't even thought about Buck for a whole week. An all-time record. Maybe now he was madly in love with her. Maybe her strategy of waiting for things to come to her had finally worked and . . .

Cary giggled. "Guess who stares at *you* that way?"

"Buck!" Sienna blurted. "I knew it! I knew it! Someday he would—"

"Oh, Sienna. Get real." Jess rolled her eyes.

"Then who?" She frowned.

"Wow." Cary turned to Jess. "She hasn't noticed."

"Would you two cut it out? Tell me!"

"Go home," said Jess, "and put your videotape of the China Hill press conference in the VCR. You did tape it, I presume."

"Of course," answered Sienna.

Cary nodded. "Watch it closely. Take a look at who's looking at you."

Sienna stood up and faced her friends. "I am not going home to look at that tape, because you are going to tell me right here and right now exactly who you are talking about."

"*Two* of them," said Jess.

"Huh?" Sienna felt more confused than ever.

Cary giggled again. "Your two lover boys. Your wanna-be boyfriends."

"Two? Who?"

"You sound like an owl." Jess chuckled.

"Somebody likes me? Tell me! Pleee-ease!"

Cary yawned. "Ho-hum. Well, probably lots of boys like you, Sienna. You're friendly and pretty—"

Sienna tapped her foot. "You have three seconds. One . . . two . . ."

"We'll give you clues," said Jess. "Bachelor number one. Tall, blond—"

"Radical, tie-dye . . ." added Cary.

"Oh, my gosh!" Sienna cried. "Not—"

Jess nodded. "Initials F.S."

"That's impossible." Sienna shook her head. "Freedom can't stand me. He's always ragging on me about one thing or another."

"And guess who else," Jess challenged.

Sienna made a face. "I'm not sure I want to. This is bad enough already."

"Bachelor number two," said Cary. "Um, talkative, outgoing . . ."

Jess snickered. "Energetic, annoying . . ."

Sienna widened her eyes in horror. "It can't be."

Cary snapped her fingers and started singing. "S.S. and R.S., sittin' in a tree. K-I-S-S-I—"

"Stop!" Sienna covered her ears. But she couldn't help grinning. "This is just too ridiculous. *Ramon?*"

"Could be worse," offered Jess by way of comfort.

Sienna crossed her arms. "I doubt it."

"Then why are you smiling?" asked Cary.

"Because . . . because . . ." Sienna thought for a minute. "Because this is an important moment in my life. A stage of adolescence. A rite of passage. Part of becoming an adult."

"In other words?" asked Cary.

"In other words," she began, trying to be serious.

109

She bit her lip and frowned, but the giggles burst out anyway. "Somebody—no, *two* somebodies—like me!"

The idea made her feel nervous and silly and very, very good.

Sienna dashed the half block home. She couldn't wait to tell her parents all about it. Not one, but *two* boys liked her. According to Jess and Cary, anyway.

Of course, neither boy qualified as a Prince Charming. She certainly had no interest in them as *boyfriends*. But what an important stage this was, if her friends were right. Maybe she was already becoming a teenager, even though her thirteenth birthday was still three months away.

Should she just come right out and ask the boys? *Excuse me, Ramon, do you have a crush on me?* Too uncool. Get someone else to ask them? *Hmm.* They probably wouldn't admit it, anyway. Boys were tricky. She sighed. No matter. She didn't mind staying in suspense. The mystery just added to the excitement, which was part of being a teenager. In the surviving adolescence seminar the instructor had talked about the emotional ups and downs experienced by all teens and how important they were to growth and development. Well, here we go! thought Sienna.

''Mom!'' she called, throwing open the condo's front door. ''Mom!''

"In here," Dad answered from the kitchen.

"Hi! You'll never guess what—" Sienna stopped short.

Her parents sat on bar stools at opposite ends of the counter, looking very serious.

Sienna's stomach turned a flip. Her mouth went dry. *Oh, no.* This must be it. The moment she had dreaded.

"Come in, darling. Sit down," said Mom.

Dad pulled up a bar stool for her.

"I didn't mean to interrupt." Sienna shook her head. "I'll just—"

"No, no." Mom patted the bar stool seat.

"We'd like to talk with you," Dad assured her. "We were waiting for you."

With her heart in her throat, Sienna sat between them.

"Your mother and I have reached a decision."

Maybe, thought Sienna, if she just put everything in reverse, retraced her steps, ran back to Cary's house, she could make this moment never happen.

Mom sighed. "Dad and I have done a lot of talking. We feel very good about what we've decided. Next month, your aunt Anna is going to stay with you."

Both Mom and Dad would leave the house! Time apart meant time apart from *her,* too! Sienna felt weak.

"While your mother and I," continued Dad, "spend time alone together."

The pounding thrum of worry in Sienna's head was so loud that several seconds passed before she heard it.

"We'll drive to Santa Fe, which is where Dad and I first met," her mother went on, "for a vacation together. Two weeks."

"Together?" Sienna repeated.

Dad took her hand. "We're sorry to leave you behind, Sienna, but—"

"No," she interrupted, "really, that's fine. That's great. Fabulous! Together. Wow! Not time apart?"

Mom shook her head. "There must be a reason why we could never agree to do that. It's just not what we want. We started to feel the opposite, in fact, that we need more time together. But in a different environment, without the day-to-day questions and pressures that crop up. You understand that it's not *you,* though, don't you, darling? We certainly aren't trying to get away from you. We just need some space to work things out on our own."

"Hey, no problem!" Sienna chirped. Her world was coming right-side up again. "Are you kidding? This is *wonderful!*"

"Hmm." Dad rubbed his knees, grinning. "Sounds like somebody's looking forward to getting rid of us, doesn't it, Liv?"

Mom laughed. "That is what it sounds like."

"Oh, yeah, right!" Sienna rolled her eyes. "Like, I'm really looking forward to living with Aunt Anna. Last time she stayed with me she made me set my alarm fifteen minutes early so I'd be ready the second Jess and Cary got here. She rearranged my closet, moved Number One's litter box to the garage, and we had frozen diet entrees every night for dinner."

"I'm sure there are worse fates than spending a couple of weeks with my sister," said Dad.

Sienna nodded and reached her arms out to include both him and Mom in a big family hug. Two weeks with Aunt Anna? She could handle a lot worse than that, now that her parents' time apart had turned into time together.

At school the next day she kept a sharp eye out. How, exactly, did boys act when they liked a girl? The more she thought about it, the more interesting things she remembered about Freedom's and Ramon's behavior toward her. For instance, the worried look on Ramon's face the day she yelled at him for dropping out of the tree to say hello. Worried was a very new look for Ramon. Usually he enjoyed getting on people's nerves. Maybe, that day, he had actually wanted to talk to her. And then there was the time when Freedom tried to get her to join the Save China Hill committee. Other times, it seemed he couldn't decide how to act toward her, going back and forth between being rude and being polite. Boys were weird.

Nothing particularly weird happened at school Thursday. But when she got home in the afternoon the phone was ringing. *Hello, Freedom,* she imagined saying. *Yes, let's talk about your feelings for me.*

"Ulterior Designs," she answered with the name of her mother's company.

"Well, hello, Sienna. Remember me?"

The voice was certainly not a boy's. "Oh, Mrs. Pollard! Hello!"

"You do remember. How are you, dear? Your mother and I chat about you every time she comes to work on my house. Oh, and you should see what she's done here, Sienna. My house is indeed turning into a home. Why don't you come with her sometime? I'd love to see you."

"Thank you, Mrs. Pollard. I'd like that. Mom says she's having fun doing your house."

"We both are. She's delightful. Well, is she home this afternoon?"

"No," Sienna answered. "She had some appointments, I think. Can I take a message?"

"If you would, dear, ask her to call me when she has a moment. I found the family photographs she wanted and thought she'd like to know. I believe she's going to do a portrait hall or something for me. Your mother is so creative, one never knows what she'll come up with."

Sienna laughed. "That's for sure. Well, I'll tell her you called, Mrs. Pollard."

"Thank you, dear. By the way, how has your connection with Arthur Kingston worked out? Has he been helpful to your club or a bother?"

"A bother? No, he's very nice. And he tried to help, but . . ." Suddenly, one of Mrs. Pollard's words flashed brightly in Sienna's mind.

"But what, dear?"

Connection, thought Sienna. Why hadn't she thought of this before? "Well, we keep hitting brick walls everywhere. And now that you mention it, Mrs. Pollard, I was wondering . . ." Sienna kept thinking. The other day Webb had said Moreland and Mortimer had connections with powerful people. Well, so did the Eco-kids. "Mrs. Pollard, do you think you might be able to help us?"

"In what way? If it's a donation you need—"

"Actually, it's not. What we really need, I think, is *you.*"

"Me?" Mrs. Pollard laughed. "As a volunteer?"

"Yes." Sienna decided to plunge right in. "See, you're rich and that probably means people pay attention to you, doesn't it?"

Another laugh. "My dear, your frankness is refreshing. Do I understand that you want me to get someone's attention for you?"

"Exactly! Could you? We can't seem to get anywhere at all on saving China Hill, and—"

"Whose attention does your club need, Sienna?"

"I think . . ." Sienna made a quick decision. "Could you help us get through to the company that wants to build up there? It's called Moreland and Mortimer."

"Moreland and Mortimer?" Mrs. Pollard repeated. "Is that so? Well, just a moment, dear. Let me look something up."

Sienna heard pages rustling, as if Mrs. Pollard were flipping through an address book.

"Yes, just as I thought. I should have no trouble at all arranging a meeting between your group and the company's top executives."

"Really?" Sienna nearly fell over.

"Well, Kendall Kirstner is the architect who designed my house," said Mrs. Pollard, "and he is also the architect for Moreland and Mortimer. Ken is a dear boy, almost like a nephew to me now. I'll just have a word with him."

Sienna heard more pages flipping.

"Oh, and isn't this something? Just as I thought. Norrie Robb is the company president, isn't she?"

Norrie? wondered Sienna.

"My brother played polo with her father for many

years at the Pine Club.'' Mrs. Pollard remembered. ''And her mother and I took swimming lessons together.''

''Really?'' Sienna wondered if ''that girl'' Norrie Robb meant the blond in a business suit, Nora Robb, who had ruined the Eco-kids press conference.

''I understand she's a powerful business leader now,'' Mrs. Pollard went on. ''I'll have a little chat with her, why don't I, and invite her to a meeting with your club. You could all come here, to my home, for tea. Neutral territory.''

''You would do that?'' asked Sienna.

''Of course I would.'' Mrs. Pollard sounded amused. ''And I will. I'm quite the diplomat, you know. I enjoy this sort of thing. Getting people together, ironing things out. And I've had a good deal of success at it. I like to think it's my charming personality.''

This time Sienna laughed. ''*I* like your personality, Mrs. Pollard.''

''Thank you, dear. I'll be in touch with you about this soon, all right?''

''All right! This is great! Thanks, Mrs. Pollard!''

Sienna hung up, humming. What exactly would the Eco-kids say to Nora Robb? She had no idea. How could they, a bunch of kids, get a powerful business leader to change her mind? She'd better call Cary right away.

Cary wasn't home, and before she could try again, Mandy came over. For a while they played with Number One, then Mandy invited Sienna to her house to play Ping-Pong.

They were halfway down the block when Sienna spotted a group of people on the sidewalk in front of Cary's house.

"Mind if we see what's going on?" she asked Mandy. "I've got to tell Cary something anyway."

Mandy shrugged. As they got closer Sienna saw some neighbors, Penny Allbright and Joel Sobieski, along with Cary, Jess, Mr. Kingston with a big tan-colored dog, and two people with binoculars hanging from their necks.

"Hi, everybody!" Sienna said. "Oh, you must be Gem!" She pet Mr. Kingston's dog, who wiggled mightily, slapping Sienna's legs with her tail.

"You ought to come, too." Mr. Kingston pointed at Sienna.

"Me? Come where?"

"To China Hill," said the woman with binoculars. Tall and sturdy, she had short, graying hair, thick glasses, and a strong resemblance to the man with binoculars.

"Gotta show you," said the man, a much-older version of the woman. He leaned on a cane and his glasses were so thick that Sienna could barely see his eyes. He wore a green baseball cap with a brown pelican stitched onto it.

Jess shook her head. "We can't go out on China Hill. It says No Trespassing."

"We won't go in very far," the woman promised, "and we won't do any harm. My father spotted something important there." She nodded at the older man. "Come take a look. I think you'll appreciate it, considering your efforts to protect the area."

118

Sienna, Jess, and Cary exchanged glances. For her part, Sienna was terribly curious. What could this be?

Penny looked at the girls. "I'll come with you, if you like." She was one of Sienna's favorite neighbors. She probably sensed that they felt funny about going beyond that sign *and* going there with strangers.

"Sorry, I've got to get back to my kids," said Mr. Sobieski, waving toward the two toddlers on his front lawn next door, "but keep me posted, all right? My wife and I are standing by to help you get a petition going."

Cary nodded. "Thanks."

"Do you want to go to China Hill?" Sienna whispered to Mandy.

"Well ..." Mandy grinned a little. "I do like mysteries."

"Okay," Cary told Mr. Kingston. "But we won't stay there long."

On the way down the street, with Gem trotting at the end of her leash, Mr. Kingston introduced the people who wore binoculars. "This is Rhoda Kramer and her father, Bob. Bob and I play pool down at the senior center. Couple days ago I told him about this China Hill thing, and he told me they can't possibly put houses there. Then he takes me out there and shows me why. You'll see in just a minute, girls."

Near Mandy's house at the end of Opal Street, they made a right on Emerald Drive. Sienna could hear the soft roar of the surf below the houses.

She could also hear the steady clip-clop of Penny's clogs on the sidewalk in front of her and the swish of her long, hippie-style skirt. A long brown braid ran down Penny's back. It sure was nice to have the young woman around. Sienna felt much better about invading China Hill with an adult they knew. At Ruby Lane they turned left, and after just a few houses the lane dead-ended on Diamond Court.

"Well, here's one thing I wanted to show you," said Mr. Kingston. He pointed at a huge old house in serious need of paint and a new roof. The front yard was weedy and overgrown. "Louis Gentry's house. He inherited it from his grandmother a few years ago. Old Mrs. Rutherford loved her roses, but they're gone now. Gentry let the place go to ruin. He talked big at first, and that's how we elected him to head our neighborhood group. Cary, you asked me why he didn't show up at that press conference."

"That right. Why didn't he?" Cary frowned.

Mr. Kingston sighed. "He's gone."

"Out of town?" asked Jess.

"Moved," answered Mr. Kingston. "Lady next door to him told me. Said he up and sold his house."

"Really?" Sienna raised an eyebrow. "Now there's a mystery for you, Mandy. The guy said he was going to help us. He was even president of the homeowners association, and—"

"Wait a minute," Penny interrupted. "Louis Gentry. Blond guy? Smiles a lot?"

"A lot," Jess confirmed.

Penny nodded. "I think I know him. He's a client at the law firm I work for. He had an appointment there just last week, in fact. You say he's the one who talked you into the press conference?"

"Then disappeared," added Cary.

"Hmm." Penny frowned, thinking.

120

They walked past Mr. Gentry's house to the China Hill bluff right next door. Gem pranced and whined.

"She loves to run here," Mr. Kingston explained, petting his dog. "Now, now, Gemmie, simmer down."

"I'm afraid you'll have to keep her on leash," Rhoda warned him, "and keep her very quiet, if we're going to see what we're here for."

"Yes, of course. Did you hear that, Gemmie? Stay quiet, now."

Rhoda and her father led the way past the No Trespassing sign without so much as a glance at it.

Jess checked her watch. "It's four thirty-five. We're not going to stay here long, right?"

"Right," answered Bob over his shoulder. "Quiet, now."

He and his daughter crept slowly down a narrow path that Sienna had never tried before. It wound through the low, golden brush that blanketed China Hill. Once in a while Sienna looked out at the sea, today calm and baby blue. Through clear skies she saw the bridges in San Diego and the hills of Mexico to the south. In an hour the sun would set. Sunsets on China Hill made you feel like you owned the world. But if Moreland and Mortimer got their way, the bluff would be covered with town houses and only the people who bought them could enjoy the views.

"Hey, a whale!" Cary pointed offshore, where a misty fountain sprayed up from the waves.

"Thar she blows!" cried Mr. Kingston.

The Kramers pulled up their binoculars.

"Can you see the whale?" Mandy asked them.

121

Rhoda shook her head. "It must have dived down. But there's a blow from another one."

"What we're seeing," Jess explained from behind Sienna, "is the whale's moist breath exhaled from the blowhole on top of his head. It's probably a California gray whale, the most common species here this time of year. They're on their way back north to the Arctic after spending the winter south in Mexico."

"Is this what you wanted to show us?" Cary asked the Kramers. She stood next to them. "We've seen whales before."

"Patience," said Mr. Kingston from behind Mandy.

"Just a little further," Bob promised, "then we'll stop and wait for a while."

"Wait for wh—" Penny began, and then had to unfasten her skirt, which was snagged on a sagebrush. "The girls did say they don't want to spend too much time here, and I'm a bit worried about it, myself. This isn't public—"

"Shh!" Rhoda pulled up her binoculars again.

"He's here!" whispered Bob.

They crouched low and peered into the brush a few yards off. Sienna didn't see a thing. But after a moment she heard mewing.

"Kittens?" Sienna whispered. "Do they want us to rescue kittens again?"

Jess turned around and shrugged. "If it is a kitten, it's a good thing Gem is back there with Mr. Kingston."

Rhoda passed her binoculars to Cary and pointed into the brush. "Do you see him? It's a male. You can tell by the black cap."

Bob passed his binoculars to Jess. "Take a look."

122

"Hey, I see it!" whispered Mandy. "Look! There!"

Sienna caught a glimpse of something. A flutter of gray. "A bird?"

She heard the mewing again, three soft notes rising and falling.

"Not just any bird," Jess corrected.

"Are you familiar with it?" asked Rhoda. "Hear the call?"

Jess handed the binoculars to Penny. "It's the coastal California gnatcatcher."

"Right." Bob smiled. "How'd you know? You a birder?"

Jess shook her head. "No. I read an article about it in a nature magazine."

"That little guy's going to save this bluff!" crowed Mr. Kingston. He moved up and clapped Bob on the back. "Thanks to you bird-watchers!"

The excitement made Gem start whining again.

"Shh!" Rhoda frowned.

"Quiet, now, Gemmie!" ordered Mr. Kingston. The dog gave one last whimper in protest then leaned against him for a backrub.

Penny snapped her fingers. "Oh, I remember. The gnatcatcher. It's been in the newspaper. An endangered species?"

A grin appeared on Rhoda's face for the first time all afternoon. "It made it to the threatened species list."

"You're happy about that?" Sienna frowned. "Happy that it might go extinct?"

"What we're happy about is that he's *here!*" said Mr. Kingston. "That little bird is going to help us."

"How?" asked Mandy.

123

Penny handed the binoculars to Sienna. "Before a developer builds on any piece of property, they have to show it won't harm the environment. At least, not too much. Well, if they find a plant or animal that's in danger of becoming extinct—"

Mandy cut in with, "You mean, there aren't many of them left?"

"Right," said Bob. "Experts say there might only be a few thousand California gnatcatchers left."

Sienna held her breath. The little bird she found in the binoculars was smaller than a sparrow. It was pudgy and cute. At the same time it looked very distinguished in its blue-gray feather suit, with a lighter gray chest, a black cap, and black tail. Perched in a low bush, it pecked something off a leaf.

"Does it really catch gnats?" asked Mandy.

Rhoda nodded. "Insects and bugs are most of its diet, including beetles, wasps, ants, flies, spiders. . . . It helps control those populations, making it an important part of the ecosystem."

"The development company can't build here," said Cary, "now that you've found gnatcatchers, right?"

"Well, it makes it harder for them," said Rhoda. "They have to prove that they won't disturb the birds' nesting efforts."

Sienna's heart sank. "You mean they might still be able to put the town houses up?" She watched the bird hop from branch to branch, its bright eyes searching for things to eat. It kept making that kittenlike mewing chirp. What if bulldozers came roaring through its home?

"We're reporting these sightings of the gnatcatcher

124

to our local bird-watching organizations," said Rhoda. "By law, the development company will not be able to build anything here unless they can show they won't do the birds any harm. And this piece of property is so small, it would be awfully hard for them to carry on construction without disturbing the birds."

"Can I see?" asked Mandy.

Sienna handed her the binoculars.

"Oh, he's adorable!" Mandy cried. "Is it really true that he and others like him might just die out? There would be no more of them?"

Bob nodded. "If they don't have enough land to feed on and to raise their young, why sure. It's happened before with other critters, as we all know. This bird's habitat—"

"What's that?" asked Mr. Kingston.

"Habitat means the type of area where it lives," explained Rhoda. "The gnatcatcher's habitat is areas just like this bluff here—dry slopes close to the ocean. But humans have taken over most of its territory. We've built on *eighty percent* of these bluffs."

"We need to keep China Hill in the twenty percent that's left," said Jess.

"We sure do!" echoed Cary.

"Hello there, birdie," Penny chirped. "You know what? I think you've joined the Eco-kids."

Sienna nodded. "And I know just how you can attend your first meeting."

11

Mrs. Pollard's living room was at least three times the size of any living room Sienna had ever seen. One wall was all floor-to-ceiling windows facing the ocean, with several sets of French doors leading out to the lawn where the auction had been held. Polished wood floors gleamed in the afternoon light.

Sienna knew from the moment she walked in that her mother had "done" the room. Mom always let her clients' tastes shine through instead of her own, but who else but Liv Engstrom would think of dressing two armchairs as a man and a woman, complete with a button-front jacket and Derby hat for the "man," and a ruffled calico dress for the "woman."

"Have another scone, Norrie, won't you?" Mrs. Pollard was the perfect hostess. While two maids offered food and poured tea, she chatted with her guests and helped everyone feel at home.

Despite Mrs. Pollard's efforts to seat everyone together, the Eco-kids and their friends had gathered on one side of the fireplace, and the representatives from Moreland and Mortimer stayed on the other.

"Sienna," Mom whispered, catching her daughter's

126

sleeve, "I'm going to sit quietly in a corner and not say a word unless you ask me to, all right?"

Sienna nodded, hoping Mom wouldn't say anything more. How embarrassing if her friends figured out that her mother was attending the meeting as a bodyguard.

"One run-in with Moreland and Mortimer is enough," Dad had insisted when he found out about the upcoming meeting at Mrs. Pollard's.

"We're not going to let you face them alone this time," Mom had chimed in.

Sienna protested that she'd be anything but alone, what with the whole Save China Hill committee and Mr. Kingston and the Kramers and even Mrs. Pollard around, but secretly she was happy to have her mother there, too.

The antique clock over the fireplace read ten till four, giving her a jitters attack worse than she'd ever had before a dance or drama performance.

"I hope we're ready for this." Cary settled in next to her on a big pink sofa. "Did you bring the report, Jess?"

Sitting on the other side, Jess answered by pointing to a thick stack of papers in her lap. "And the Kramers have done the bird research. . . ."

They glanced at Bob and Rhoda sitting with Mr. Kingston nearby. Webb and Freedom flanked them in the dressed-up chairs.

Hallie walked up looking panicked. "Where's Penny? She's supposed to have the legal information."

Cary glanced at the clock. "Well, she said she might be a little late."

"Relax, you guys." Sienna shook her head. "*I'm* the

127

one who has to do the talking, remember? I've got a right to be nervous!''

''Oh, there's Penny!'' said Mr. Kingston.

She walked in wearing her usual long skirt and braided hair. Sienna noticed Nora Robb frowning at Penny's Birkenstocks from the other side of the room. The brown-suited man next to Nora darted his gaze nervously about. He reminded Sienna of a chipmunk.

Penny hurried over and squatted in front of the girls. ''I've got to tell you something before this thing starts.'' She lowered her voice. ''Guess what Louis Gentry was up to.''

Sienna leaned forward. Webb and Freedom gathered closer.

''Remember that Mr. Kingston said Gentry recently sold his house? And remember where Gentry's property happens to be? Well, I had a hunch about it and—''

Webb widened his eyes. ''He sold it to Moreland and Mortimer?''

''You got it.'' Penny grinned.

Sienna shook her head. ''But why—''

The antique clock chimed four.

''Well, shall we begin our meeting now?'' Mrs. Pollard asked from the center of the room. ''I think we're all present and ready, aren't we? Moreland and Mortimer Corporation's president, Ms. Nora Robb, would like to say a few words to begin, if that's all right with the Eco-kids.'' She turned to Sienna.

''Oh, yes, that's fine,'' Sienna agreed.

''Thank you,'' said Ms. Robb, standing up. ''There are some points I wanted to clarify for us all.'' She smiled.

Mom caught Sienna's eye and winked. Sienna looked away, hoping her mother didn't keep this up during the whole meeting.

"Let me make some introductions. I'm Nora Robb, and this is Moreland and Mortimer's community outreach director, Don Simms." She gestured at the chipmunk man. "Our company is committed to bringing quality homes into the lives of Americans. We want you wonderful Eco-kids to know that we believe that quality includes preserving the earth for future generations."

Although she tried to pay attention, Sienna's mind kept drifting back to Penny's news. Louis Gentry had sold his house to Moreland and Mortimer. Why? It felt like the missing piece of a puzzle, but Sienna wasn't even sure what the puzzle was. She wished she could ask Penny.

"So . . ." Ms. Robb still wore her pasted-on smile. "I want you to know that we are here today to let you know that the Moreland and Mortimer Development Corporation is looking forward to being a part of your community. And we'll answer any questions you may have today."

It's about time, Sienna wanted to say. Nora Robb's company had ignored the Eco-kids' phone calls for weeks. If there was one thing Sienna hated, it was being ignored.

"Thank you, Nora," said Mrs. Pollard. "Now, Sienna?"

Her heartbeat picked up. It was time to jump in. She had gone over her notecards so many times that she hardly needed them anymore. Not only did she remember exactly what the Save China Hill committee wanted her to say, but she had practiced and practiced until she found just the right way to say it. Slowly, steadily, building up to a dramatic climax that would amaze her audience, just like any other good performance.

Sienna stood up. "Thanks for coming to talk with us, Ms. Robb and Mr. Simms. We do have some questions for you." She made eye contact with them. "First of all, we've been wondering how you're going to fit twelve town houses on China Hill, along with the picnic and recreation areas you've talked about. The bluff seems small for all that."

Ms. Robb pointed at her briefcase. The chipmunk man opened it and pulled out a map. He held it up while Ms. Robb described what would go where. "There will be three rows of town houses, each on a different terraced level of the bluff. So you see, there's really plenty of space."

"You'll be clearing away all the sagebrush at the top of the bluff, then, since that's where the first row of town houses will go?" asked Sienna.

"Our policy at Moreland and Mortimer is to touch the natural landscape as little as possible," Ms. Robb answered. "There will be some clearing, of course, but some of the brush will remain."

"Some, but not much, right?"

Mr. Simms smiled. "We've already addressed these issues in the environmental report we made in order to get our building permit. The government reviewed our report and granted us the permit. They're satisfied that we're going to keep China Hill beautiful, and so are we."

"The environmental report?" repeated Sienna. "Oh, yes, we have it right here."

Mr. Simms blinked. "How did you get that?"

Sienna turned to Cary, who shrugged. "Same way anyone else can. It's in the government files. My mom took me to the civic center downtown and we ordered a copy. The Eco-kids paid for the copying costs with money we've made from our school and neighborhood recycling." She grinned proudly.

"How resourceful." Ms. Robb smiled.

"Yes," agreed Sienna. "Then Jess, our science expert, went over the report. She found that it doesn't include all the information it should."

Mr. Simms laughed out loud. "That's a very long and complex report. There's no way a child can understand—"

Ms. Robb interrupted. "We hired the best scientists in the city to make that report. It's very thorough."

"There's nothing wrong with that report." Mr. Simms fidgeted with his pen.

Sienna felt a rush of delight. What fun it was to turn the tables. A few weeks ago Moreland and Mortimer had put the Eco-kids on the defense at the press conference. Now it was *their* time to squirm.

"We found something missing," Sienna said.

Ms. Robb frowned. "Which is?"

"The coastal California gnatcatcher!" Rhoda blurted. She wasn't supposed to say anything, but Sienna knew the woman just couldn't help herself when it came to birds.

The Moreland and Mortimer people looked blank.

Too blank, thought Sienna. Maybe even blank on purpose.

"Yes," Sienna said, "the coastal California gnatcatcher."

A sense of power zinged through her blood. When you know you're right, she realized, you know exactly what to do. Nothing can stop you.

That was what she had lacked at the press conference, when she hadn't yet decided how she felt about protecting China Hill. Now, though, she locked her eyes on Ms. Robb and Mr. Simms.

"There aren't many of these gnatcatchers left," she told them, "because their habitat has been cut down so much. They nest on bluffs just like China—"

"Let me just explain—" Ms. Robb interrupted.

Sienna interrupted right back. "Eighty percent of their habitat is gone. It's been built on or destroyed by humans in other ways. These small, pretty birds have very few places to live now."

Cary held up a photo of the gnatcatcher in one of Bob Kramer's bird books.

"This bird," said Sienna, "is just one of the animals and plants that your building project might harm. The gnatcatcher is important not just on its own, but also because it represents all the things we lose whenever places like China Hill get built on. If we keep going on this way, pretty soon there will be no place for rabbits and coyotes and flowers and bugs to live, either. There will be no place for us humans to see beauty and feel harmony. We *need* nature, Ms. Robb and Mr. Simms. Don't take it away from us."

For a moment there was silence. Sienna thought she heard her mother sniffle, but didn't dare look.

Mr. Simms shook his head. "Great speech. But I think that if you were to read the report properly, you'd see that it deals with these issues, and the government is satisfied with our plan."

"Jess?" Sienna turned to her friend. "Will you explain what you found in the environmental report that Mr. Simms is talking about?"

Jess read from her pocket notebook. "The report says that China Hill is a possible gnatcatcher habitat but that none were sighted."

"Exactly," agreed Ms. Robb. "None were sighted." She clasped her hands in front of her as if done with the matter.

"The interesting thing is . . ." Sienna looked across the room at her opponents. "Gnatcatchers *have* been sighted there."

"Impossible!" cried Mr. Simms.

"Saw 'em myself." Bob shrugged. "So have other birders."

"Birders are very serious about their birding," Rhoda put in. "Don't try to tell us what we did or did not see. The sightings have been officially recorded with local bird-watching organizations."

Ms. Robb went pale. Mr. Simms loosened his necktie. Sienna almost felt sorry for them. It looked like they both needed a strong cup of tea.

"You can't build on China Hill," Sienna said matter-of-factly. "Penny, would you explain the legal part?"

Penny nodded and tossed her braid over a shoulder. "The law requires you to report any new environmental information you receive about the property where you want to build. The government will have to reconsider your permit.''

Ms. Robb seemed to have collected herself. Her voice was smooth again. ''We have no qualms whatsoever about that. We've dealt with exactly the same situation before. We can build around the gnatcatcher nest sites so that we don't disturb them. The law allows that.''

Rhoda frowned. ''It's very difficult to avoid disturbing them. A nesting pair can be frightened away by noise, by bright lights, by—''

''Oh, yes, we've dealt with this before.'' Ms. Robb was smug. ''We might have to rearrange the site a bit, but—''

''Rearrange the site?'' Hallie repeated.

Ms. Robb nodded slowly, as if suddenly remembering that she was talking to children. ''We'll just put our buildings where they won't disturb the birds.''

''You can't do that!'' Freedom jumped up, shaking his fist.

Hallie pulled him down.

But then Bob Kramer took up the fight. ''You can't avoid disturbing the birds in a habitat that small. It's only a couple of acres—barely enough for one pair of birds to feed on and raise their young.''

Mr. Simms was shaking his head. ''We work within the law. We obey the law. That's all we have to do. The law has allowed us to build on this kind of location before, with gnatcatchers present, and I'm sure it will again.''

Sienna's spirits sank. She glanced at her mother, who wore a very obvious scowl aimed at the company peo-

134

ple. It looked like she wanted to do more than scowl—to jump up and give them a solid, motherish scolding. But this time, Sienna didn't want her mother or Mr. Kingston or anyone else to rescue her. She had to figure out how to handle this herself.

Something kept nagging at her, an idea she couldn't quite pin down. The Eco-kids had found pieces of a puzzle, but how did they fit in?

"Well," Ms. Robb was saying, "if we've answered all your questions . . ."

"Actually, not yet." Sienna decided to play a wild card. "There's something we've been wondering about." She tapped her fingers on her knees. "Louis Gentry sold his property to you, right? It's next door to China Hill."

She was winging it, barely knowing what she'd say next. But if shaking Ms. Robb and Mr. Simms up again was what she had wanted, that was exactly what she achieved.

"*You* bought Gentry's land?" Mr. Kingston croaked.

Ms. Robb frowned. "I beg your pardon, but that's hardly any concern of yours."

"Why, it sure is!" Mr. Kingston protested. "That's my neighborhood up there, and I have a right to know what's going on. Besides which, now I understand what that rascal was up to!"

Sienna smiled. The whole thing finally began to make sense. The puzzle pieces fell into place.

Mr. Simms shook his head. "I think this discussion has moved into an area that—"

"Oh, don't you give me that highfalutin talk!" snapped Mr. Kingston. "You know what you were up to, getting Louis Gentry to bring those kids out to a press conference. He set them out there like sitting ducks so that you could shoot at 'em. And what irks me is that I helped him! I should have known.''

Mrs. Pollard hadn't said a word before. Now she rose from her chair near the windows. "What is this all about, Nora?''

Like a kid caught with her hand in the cookie jar, Ms. Robb blushed. Mr. Simms looked like he had been sent to the principal's office.

Ms. Robb cleared her throat. "I'm not exactly sure. Would you handle this one, Don?''

Passing the buck, thought Sienna.

"Well ... uh, we simply asked Mr. Gentry to help us open up a dialog with these children.'' He looked at the Eco-kids and smiled. "To, uh, to help us talk with you.''

"Help you *what?*'' Hallie blurted. "We tried calling you for weeks. Why didn't you talk to us then?''

Mr. Kingston snorted and turned to Mrs. Pollard. "I'll explain this to you, Rowena. Here's what these company people did. Louis Gentry wanted to make some bucks off his grandmother's land. He bides his time, gets himself elected president of our neighborhood association so we'll trust him. These people come along and want to build on China Hill, and he's in a prime position to sell them his property *and* get the neighborhood to go along with the building idea.''

"But he talked like an environmentalist,'' Cary remembered glumly, "like he wanted to protect China Hill.''

Webb shook his head. "He lied to us.''

"What you're saying," Nate wondered, "is that he got us to hold that press conference so that—"

Sienna finished for him. "So that *they*"—she pointed at the Moreland and Mortimer people—"could make the Eco-kids look ridiculous."

"Yup." Mr. Kingston nodded. "They brought those people out to say they wanted construction jobs or to buy homes up there—"

"Wait just a minute," countered Mr. Simms. "Those individuals really do want jobs and homes. People want to see China Hill developed. That's a fact you just can't accept, can you?"

"We know the facts, Mr. Simms," Hallie shot back. "The fact is that saving the environment *creates* more jobs than it takes away. I have this article right here . . ." She pulled a newspaper clipping from her pocket. "People can get jobs recycling, making equipment that keeps factories from polluting, and installing solar heating systems—"

Mr. Simms glared at her. "I never thought I'd see the day when radical maniac kids would try to stand in the way of progress here in Jewel Beach. Well, we intend to see to it that—"

"Be quiet, Mr. Simms."

A hush fell over the room when everyone heard the grim tone in Mrs. Pollard's voice.

"What I've seen today is adults acting like children, and children acting like adults."

She walked slowly to the wall of windows looking out over the sea. The sheer white curtains beside her fluttered in a light breeze.

Although Mrs. Pollard kept her back to the room,

137

Sienna saw her shoulders rise and fall with a deep, pained-looking sigh. Then she turned quickly around. "I am appalled by Moreland and Mortimer's behavior in this matter. And so should you be." She nailed the two company executives with her eyes. "And I want to know right now what you are going to do to atone for it."

Ms. Robb leaned back in her chair, pale as butter again. Mr. Simms looked as shaky as if a bomb had dropped.

On the other side of the room, Sienna found a lot of smiles, including a big, proud one on her mother.

"It is quite obvious to me," added Mrs. Pollard, not yet finished with her targets, "that Moreland and Mortimer will *not* proceed with its plans for China Hill."

12

Weeks and weeks of practice boiled down to nothing but wobbly knees and sweaty palms. In barely an hour Sienna would step out onstage in front of hundreds of people attending the spring song and dance recital.

She peered one-eyed into the dressing room mirror, trying with a shaky hand to paint a streak of green over her eyelid.

"How do I look?" Mandy's reflection appeared in the mirror.

Sienna turned around. "Adorable. There's a pin sticking out of your hair, though."

Mandy leaned toward the mirror and plunged the hairpin in further. She wore painted-on whiskers, pink felt ears, and a gray bodysuit for her role in a scene from the musical *Cats*. "I like your costume a lot better. At least it's got color."

"Definitely," agreed Sienna. "Queen of the Flowers has got to have color." The yellow wasn't the best shade on her, but the loose ruffled top looked perfect for flower petals. Under it she wore her green dance tights as the stem.

"In *this* outfit"— Mandy giggled—"I look more like

139

that bird, the—What was it? The gnatcatcher? More like it than a cat.''

"Just as long as the other cats don't think so," warned Sienna, giggling with her.

"Whatever happened with that bird, anyway? The last thing you told me about was the meeting at that lady's house. What did they decide afterward? Is the company going to leave the bluff alone?"

Sienna turned back to the mirror. "I'm not sure. I missed the Eco-kids general meeting because of rehearsals, but Cary and Jess said there's good news. They're going to fill me in on it after the show."

"I had fun that day when we went out on the bluff," said Mandy. "I liked it."

Sienna stopped in the middle of a brush stroke and looked at her friend. "You did?"

Mandy nodded. "Yeah. I never really thought about stuff like that before—little birds and plants and whatever that could go extinct."

"Hmm." Sienna shut her eye again and went back to painting. "Well, we're having a picnic at the beach tomorrow. To celebrate the good news, whatever it is. You could come if you wanted."

Mandy's blue eyes lit up.

"You could even join the Eco-kids," Sienna pointed out.

Mandy grinned. "Maybe I will!"

"In the meantime . . ." Sienna put the brush down and pretended to bite her nails. "Tell me we're going to survive tonight!"

Mandy's gentle pats and reassurances helped Sienna make it to the wings a little while later, but then she was on her own. While the curtain was down between scenes, she had to go out and stand alone in the middle of the stage. When the curtain came back up again that stage would be all hers for the solo.

She shut her eyes and tried to focus on breathing. *In, energy. Out, worry. In, energy. Out, worry.* But all she could do was wonder how on earth she had ever gotten herself into this.

Then, all in an instant, the curtain rose, the lights brightened, and a sea of faces appeared before her. A deep, tingling thrill chased the fear away. *In, energy! Out, worry!*

Daffodil, Queen of the Flowers had a performance to give.

"Flowers?" Sienna couldn't believe what had just been handed to her. Backstage after the show, she stood tongue-tied and awkward next to a boy wearing a shy grin.

"Flowers for a flower." He shrugged.

She buried her nose in the pink carnations, hoping to hide her happy blush. Her first flowers from a boy! And *which* boy was even more amazing.

"It's what you're supposed to do when someone's in a play or whatever," said Ramon. "You're supposed to give them flowers as congratulations."

People bustled all around them. Any second now, she knew, her parents and other friends would show up backstage. But for the moment there was only herself and a boy who had a crush on her.

"Wow. I've never gotten flowers before, except from

my grandmother when I had the mumps.'' She smiled. ''Thanks!''

Ramon shrugged again. He wore his San Diego Padres baseball cap on backward, a baggy T-shirt and shorts, and black high-top shoes—his usual look. Except that it was very *un*usual for cocky Ramon to keep his dark eyes fixed on the floor and shuffle nervously from foot to foot. *And* for him to give compliments.

''Where'd you get those?'' Suddenly there was another boy beside her. Freedom poked his nose into the bouquet. ''Smells good.'' After a glance at Ramon, he fixed his sharp blue eyes on Sienna. ''Good performance.'' He reached out for a handshake, staring at her intensely. ''Good job.''

Suddenly Sienna knew her friends had been right. She felt a blush cover her whole face. Two boys liked her! This was so interesting. Her first challenge as a teenager. Well, almost a teenager.

Next Hallie turned up and stuck her nose in the bouquet, too. ''Oh, who gave you these?''

Sienna didn't have to answer because within seconds she was surrounded by people congratulating her and clapping her on the back. Dad held his arm around her on one side and Mom on the other while Jess snapped a picture. Cary ran up and gave her a hug. Derek Han made fun of her costume, remarking that she looked like a grasshopper.

She decided to take it as a compliment. Tonight, nothing could pop her balloon. Her Daffodil scene had gone off without a hitch and earned her a curtain call. Two boys liked her and one had given her flowers. What happened next almost bowled her over.

A handsome teenage boy punched her in the arm. "Hey, kid."

"Well, hello." Mom smiled at him. "How have you been, Buck?"

"How's your car doing?" asked Dad. "I think of it as one of our neighborhood's most interesting characters."

Sienna was holding her breath. It all felt like a dream.

Buck nodded, smoothing his slicked-back hair. "Yeah. Running fine now. Which means Mom makes me play driver again. She sent me over to pick up my sister."

Cary made a face at him.

"I hear you were in the show." He looked at Sienna and socked her in the arm again, just as he might one of his buddies in a softball game. "Way to go."

The way life worked, Sienna was beginning to realize, was that sometimes what you thought you wanted wasn't nearly as good as what you actually got.

In the case of Buck Chen, for instance, her heart would probably always pound when she saw him. Maybe someday, far, far in the future, he would see her as something other than a kid. Meanwhile, who would have thought that she'd have two boys her own age following her around?

At the Eco-kids picnic Sunday, Ramon sat with her and Mandy on their beach blanket, a big switch from the days last fall when he wouldn't be caught dead at a girls' lunch table. About every two minutes she noticed Freedom staring at her from his spot on Cary and Jess's blanket nearby. A couple of times her big straw hat flew off her head and he jumped up and got it for her. She felt like a celebrity. Next they'd be asking for her autograph.

Another example of life's funny tricks was China Hill. Sienna would never have guessed how things had turned out on that project.

When they were all finished with lunch, Hallie stood up. "Mr. Kingston would like to read a letter from Moreland and Mortimer," she announced.

Rhoda Kramer raised her hand. "After that, may I read a letter, too?"

"Sure," said Hallie. "And if anyone else wants to add something, there will be plenty of time."

Penny Allbright shrugged. "I didn't bring a letter. Just chocolate chip cookies." She pulled a paper bag out of her backpack.

It nearly caused a riot. Derek and Ramon were the first to dive in. Sienna realized that when it came to chocolate chip cookies, she lagged far behind in Ramon's heart. He moved to Penny's blanket.

Mr. Kingston rose from one of the lawn chairs that he and the Kramers had brought. He cleared his throat. "It's addressed to Mrs. Pollard. I think they still want to pretend you Eco-kids don't exist."

"But we sure do!" hollered Sam Fong, and the other Eco-juniors joined in with chants of, "We showed them! Eco-kids rule!"

"Okay, quiet down, now," Hallie told them. "Let's let Mr. Kingston read."

He cleared his throat again. " 'Dear Mrs. Pollard. In response to your questions regarding the Diamond Court Town Homes, I would like to notify you that in the interest of preserving the natural beauty and ecology of our great state of California, we at Moreland and Mortimer have chosen to establish the China Hill bluff area as public park land.' "

A chorus of cheers rang out. "Hooray! All *right!*"

"Well, how fabulous!" Sienna murmured.

" 'Enclosed please find a brochure for our Diamond Court development,' " Mr. Kingston went on, " 'a cluster of nine luxury town homes with spectacular views of San Diego Bay and beyond. These town homes provide excellent investment opportunities. I'd like to take this opportunity to thank you for the interest you have expressed in this matter. I believe that you and your young friends and generations to come will appreciate the beauty of the China Hill bluff. If I may be of any further assistance to you, I'd be delighted to hear from you. All best wishes, Nora Robb. P.S. Mother sends her best.' " Mr. Kingston chuckled.

"They're still going to build up there?" asked Mandy with a frown.

Mr. Kingston jabbed a finger at the brochure. "They show it on this map. Not on the bluff. They'll build next door. Gentry's place. They've already started tearing the house down."

"Isn't it funny, how they talk as if it was their idea all along to preserve China Hill?" Cary shook her head. "As if Mrs. Pollard just 'expressed interest' in it!"

"And as if we needed them to help us appreciate the 'beauty of the China Hill bluff'!" Freedom snorted.

"What I don't get," said Nate, "is why they didn't get the picture sooner. I mean, if it was so easy to just build on Louis Gentry's land instead of China Hill, why didn't they just do that to begin with?"

Penny chuckled. "If you figure that one out, you get a prize. No one else has. But I talked to an environmental lawyer in our office, and she said those companies often work that way. They go for the big picture first, for how they might make the most money. If someone gets in their way, they try to squash them or go around them, and if that doesn't work, they go to their backup plan to build somewhere else instead and make it look like it was their idea all along."

"Sounds familiar," muttered Jess. "Reminds me of how Aquarius Marine Park handled things when we convinced them to give up the dolphins last year."

Webb nodded. "I heard some gossip from my parents along the same lines. They heard from a friend of theirs, another real estate agent, that Moreland and Mortimer bought Gentry's land to hedge their bets. So that they'd have something to fall back on if environmentalists came along and kicked up a fuss."

"Well, we sure did that, didn't we?" Vivian snickered.

"By the way," said Sienna, "why aren't we up there 'appreciating' China Hill, as Nora Robb said we should, now that it's public? Why didn't we have the picnic up there to celebrate its' being open again?"

Bob Kramer spoke up, holding his cane in the air to get attention. "Because it's *not* public yet. Or, at least, it shouldn't be."

Rhoda nodded. "That's where the letter *we* brought comes in." She stood up and adjusted her glasses, reading, " 'To the young and courageous members of the Eco-kids club. The Jewel Beach Bird-watching Society would like to extend to you hearty congratulations and

146

many thanks for almost single-handedly rescuing China Hill from permanent destruction. You stepped in on a crisis that we and other wildlife and environmental organizations had not yet acted on, and you met with impressive success. Thanks to your taking the lead, we have been able to begin work with government officials to make sure that the California gnatcatchers remain on the bluff.' ''

Rhoda looked up through her thick glasses. "Now here comes the part they asked me to explain to you. 'Biologists are studying the bluff area to learn more about the gnatcatchers and their nesting sites. Because the area is so small, it is possible that human activity of any kind, including hiking and picnicking, could disturb the birds.' ''

"I see." Jess tapped on her chin. "So *we* have to give up China Hill, too?"

"No more walks up there for my Gem?" Mr. Kingston frowned.

"Temporarily," Rhoda stressed. "I suspect that after they finish the study, we'll be allowed on the lower part of the bluff, which doesn't seem to attract the gnatcatchers."

Bob raised his cane again. "It's only for the spring-time months, anyway, when the birds are courting and raising their young. Rest of the year isn't a problem."

"We worked so hard to keep China Hill open for us," said Hallie, "and now we're keeping ourselves out."

Ramon shrugged. "Well, no pain, no gain."

"There's a lot of gain, if we help those little birds." Mandy's blue eyes turned up toward the bluff.

Cary nodded. "So what if we miss out on a few hikes

147

and picnics up there? That's not what the Eco-kids is about, anyway.''

"To the Eco-kids!'' said Penny, raising a cookie high in a toast to them, "On a job well done!''

Mr. Kingston frowned. "Wait. I never finished my news.''

Penny shrugged and ate the cookie.

"Mrs. Pollard got an idea,'' he began. "Said she wasn't sure what you'd think of it. Might see it as us old folks trying to horn in, but . . .''

"Go ahead, Mr. Kingston,'' Hallie urged. "What's the idea?''

"Eco-seniors,'' he said simply.

"Eco-seniors?'' repeated Sienna and Freedom at the same time.

Freedom turned and gave her a smile.

"Well, you got your Eco-kids, your Eco-juniors . . . Why not let us pitch in, too?''

Cary grinned. "Wow, that's a wonderful idea, Mr. Kingston!''

"I'll be your first one,'' offered Bob Kramer.

Mr. Kingston shook his head. "Nope. Third. Rowena Pollard and I thought of it, so *we're* first and second.''

Sienna smiled. This was quite a change from the days when old Mr. Wartman next door to Cary used to yell at them for making too much noise and too much of a mess on neighborhood recycling days. Now grown-ups were arguing over who would join up first!

Glancing around at her friends, she saw old ones and new ones, young ones and old ones, the rich and not so rich, in all colors, shapes, and sizes.

So that was the trick! she suddenly realized. That was

148

how they had saved China Hill! That was how they could help the whole planet! No one person or type of person could do it alone. All kinds of people were going to have to work together.

She pulled her legs into a yoga stretch position. A few yards away the Pacific Ocean's blue waves nipped at the sand. On the other side, China Hill shimmered in its golden dress of grasses and sage.

"Eco-kids, Eco-juniors, Eco-seniors," Sienna whispered. They'd make a great team. Like the wolf pack, working together. Keeping the world green. The Green Team.

She smiled, lifting her face to the sky. The springtime sun felt good.

JOIN THE ECO-KIDS CLUB!
MAKE A DIFFERENCE
IN YOUR
NEIGHBORHOOD!

Join the ECO-KIDS CLUB, and learn how to make a difference in your neighborhood. Just for joining, you'll receive a free membership package. This package includes your very own Eco-Kids Membership Card and the first issue of the Eco-Kids Newsletter (which is printed on recycled paper). In following newsletters, learn what others are doing in their neighborhoods to help the environment, and you can share your good news and ideas with others. Join today!

Mail to:

AVON BOOKS, ATT: ORDER ENTRY DEPT.
BOX 767, DRESDEN, TN 38225

(Please fill out completely)

NAME: _____ AGE: _____

ADDRESS: _____

CITY: _____

STATE:_____

ZIP CODE: _____